"You think I'm some sort of nymphomaniac!"

"Well, you're absolutely right," she continued wildly, feeling suddenly light-headed. "I'm Good-Time Alexia."

"Giving you brandy was a mistake," he muttered wryly.

"You—with your filthy mind…you've spoiled a nice quiet evening out with a nice man…. I hate you!"

"Alexia," he said, as he put a hand on her shoulder, "I—"

"Don't you touch me!" she cried hysterically, swinging her arm up to slap his face as hard as she could.

They stood glaring at each other for a moment before he gave her a hard push that sent her tumbling back on to the sofa.

"What do you think you're doing?"

"I want you!" Raphael moved to bury his mouth in the hollow of her throat, before running his lips over her golden skin to the swell of her breast.

MARY LYONS

spanish serenade

Harlequin Books

TORONTO • NEW YORK • LONDON
AMSTERDAM • PARIS • SYDNEY • HAMBURG
STOCKHOLM • ATHENS • TOKYO • MILAN

Harlequin Presents first edition August 1984
ISBN 0-373-10714-5

Original hardcover edition published in 1984
by Mills & Boon Limited

Printed in U.S.A.

CHAPTER ONE

'Man that is born of woman hath but a short time to live, and is full of misery ...' Gusts of rain-laden wind battered the black umbrella of the solitary mourner, carrying away the words of the clergyman.

Poor Luis, thought Alexia, as she gazed down at the mound of freshly dug earth beside her husband's grave. Luis who had lived such a short while, being racked by miserable pain all the time she had known him. Twenty-six is too young, she thought, with a tiny spurt of anger. What chance had he been given to lead a normal life?

Sighing, she realised that it was no good railing against the unfairness of life; but poor dear Luis— surely he deserved a better fate than the pitifully cold, dark trench awaiting his coffin? He, who had so hated the English climate, always longing for the heat of his native Spain.

Alexia gripped the handle of her umbrella as a sharp gust of wind whipped against her pale cheeks and the escaping tendrils of gold hair. Her eyes filled with tears as she looked blindly ahead while the priest concluded the service.

'Earth to earth, ashes to ashes, dust to dust ...' She closed her eyes, praying fervently for her husband's soul now happily released from his sick body.

'Mrs ... er ...' Alexia turned. The young clergyman standing awkwardly beside her gulped as he looked at the beautiful girl. Her large green eyes, curiously flecked with gold, swam with unshed tears as she tried to smile and thank him for the service. Impulsively he grasped her cold hand. 'If there's anything I can do—anything at all—please don't hesitate to let me know.'

'Thank you,' she said, in a soft low voice. 'You've been very kind.'

'Not at all, not at all. It's been my pleasure. I mean . . .' he floundered miserably, 'it's not my pleasure, of course, it's just that I'd like to help you if I possibly can.' His words were interrupted by a dry cough.

Alexia and the young clergyman turned around, startled, to see a tall figure standing the other side of the new grave.

'How very, very touching!' the stranger drawled ironically. Alexia turned her startled eyes to the priest, who looked equally mystified.

'Señora Valverde?' The man was tall, dressed in a black coat over a dark suit, his white shirt emphasising his tanned complexion. His voice, with a slight Spanish accent, grated harshly as he looked fixedly at Alexia.

'Señora *Luis* Valverde?' he repeated.

'Yes, I'm Mrs Valverde, but . . .' she hesitated. 'I don't think I . . .' Alexia took an involuntary step backward as the stranger's dark eyes suddenly blazed with anger before being swiftly masked by his heavy eyelids.

'You do not think we have met? You are quite right—we have not.' He turned to the clergyman. 'That will be all, thank you,' he said dismissively, coming forward to take Alexia's arm. 'I will see the Señora back to her car.'

It was some moments before Alexia, trying to collect her scattered wits, found herself being propelled swiftly down the path of the large London cemetery.

'Please . . .? What's going on?' she demanded in a panic as she tried to withdraw her arm which was being firmly held by the stranger's strong hand. 'Let me go. Immediately!'

'Certainly,' he said, as they arrived at her small car, which was dwarfed by the large chauffeur-driven Daimler beside it.

Trembling with shock and fright, Alexia looked up into the cold eyes of her abductor. 'What is this? Some sort of kidnapping? Just who do you think you are . . .?'

'I am Rafael Valverde. Luis was my brother—my younger brother.'

'Oh, I didn't know . . . I mean, Luis never said . . .' She was shaken and confused by the events of the last few minutes, shaking her head with perplexity as she strove to understand what the stranger was saying.

'You did not know Luis had a brother?' The man gave a grim smile. 'No, I'm sure you didn't! It would not have suited your plans, would it?'

Alexia blinked in bewilderment. 'I don't know what you're talking about.' That Luis should have had a brother seemed incredible, and one, moreover, who appeared to be so angry with her. It must all be some terrible mistake.

'Look,' she said, trying to speak calmly, despite her confused state and her rising anger at the man's intrusion into her husband's funeral, 'I'm sure there must be some mistake. You say you're Luis' brother, but if so, he never mentioned you. He told me that all his family were dead.'

The man reached inside his jacket, and for a split second she wondered if he was going to produce a gun—the afternoon had taken on such a surrealistic quality that anything was possible. In fact the stranger produced a wallet and grimly handed her a card.

'I am sorry to disappoint you, but I am indeed Luis's brother. Furthermore, his sorrowing mother and sister are very much alive, and living in Madrid!'

'I'm sorry, *señor* ... I've just buried my husband, and now ...' Alexia sighed and leant against her car. It was all too much. She just wished this angry man would go away and leave her in peace.

'I understand it must be an unpleasant shock,' he said, his eyes narrowing as he looked searchingly at the weary girl in front of him.

'A shock? Well ... yes. But unpleasant? Why should it be unpleasant? What is unpleasant,' she said sharply, 'is to be treated with such bad manners by you *señor!*' She glared at Luis's brother, who waved aside her spirited words.

'You have a child, I believe.'

'Yes, Luis's son, Juan.'

'Why is he not here to mourn his father?' The stranger's accusatory tone and arrogant, supercilious attitude made Alexia suddenly seethe with anger.

She gestured around the crowded cemetery, with its row upon row of gravestones. 'Do you really consider this a—a suitable place for a child who's only four? I would like him to have happy memories of his father, not these—these terrible surroundings.' She shivered, her anger dissolving away, leaving her feeling cold, tired and miserable.

'I understand,' he said shortly, and for a moment it seemed as if his face softened as he looked down into her eyes. However, she decided that she must have been mistaken as, glancing swiftly at his watch, he continued in the same arrogant tone he had used to her before. 'We must talk, you and I, but not now. I am late for an appointment already.'

'I can't think of anything we have to say to each

other . . .' Alexia gasped, as her arm was held firmly again by Rafael.

'Oh yes, we have, my dear sister-in-law. Indeed we have!' He gave a sardonic smile which did not reach his angry dark eyes, as he again reached into his jacket and handed her a long slim envelope. 'Here is Luis's will, which was delivered to me today. I suggest you read it carefully. I will see you tomorrow at my hotel, at six o'clock sharp.'

His bland assumption that she would just drop everything to obey his summons made her gasp with fury. 'I'm afraid it's not convenient to me,' she snapped. 'I've made other arrangements for that time.' May God forgive me for the lie, she thought, but he's the most insufferable man I've ever met!

'I think you will find it is convenient,' he said with a grim smile, as he turned to walk away to his waiting vehicle.

'Really! Of all the . . .' Alexia jumped into her car, angrily banging the door shut with fury, before driving swiftly away.

'Calm down, Alexia. I'll make us a cup of tea and you can tell me all about Luis's brother.'

'Oh, Melanie,' Alexia looked fondly at her friend, 'what would I do without you!'

'Well, you'd have a different next-door neighbour for a start!' Melanie Watson laughed, as she placed the kettle on the stove, and put the cups ready on the table. 'Seriously, though, I wish you'd let me go to the funeral with you. You shouldn't have gone on your own.'

'It was kind of you to offer, but Uncle Walter was going to come—until he woke up and looked at the weather. You know what a raving hypochondriac he is:

"You can't expect an old man like me to come out on a day like this. The worst May in living memory",' Alexia mimicked her uncle's quavering voice.

'Old man my foot! He's only fifty-five, Alexia.'

'I know that. You know that. But you try telling it to my uncle. If he comes over to have a meal, he'll never stay the night because he's afraid of damp sheets!' Alexia smiled wryly. 'Anyway, it was really better to have you here looking after Juan.' She brushed a tired hand across her forehead. 'Was he all right?'

'He was fine, absolutely no problem. You really didn't need me, you know. Anna's a real find—you never seem to have a problem with your au pair girls. Not like so many of my friends.'

'You know,' Alexia said thoughtfully, 'I felt terribly wicked when I had my first au pair girl. It seemed . . . well, so lazy somehow. Still, with Luis so ill, I had to be the breadwinner, and that meant finding someone to look after Juan.'

'Of course it did,' Melanie said soothingly. 'Now come on, sit down and drink your tea, it will do you good. How did the funeral go? Was it a nice service?'

'Yes, it was. Very simple, you know, but so cold out by the grave. The clergyman was sweet, and then . . .' Alexia gulped. 'It was so awful! This ghastly man just strode up and grabbed me, carting me off to my car like a piece of flotsam, and announced that he was Luis's brother.'

'What's he like?'

'He's quite the rudest man I've ever met! You've no idea how horrid he was. It didn't seem to matter a damn that I'd just buried poor Luis . . .' Alexia grabbed for a handkerchief and blew her nose fiercely.

'Poor love!' Melanie put an arm around the girl's thin shoulders.

'The awful thing was . . .' Alexia sniffed, 'I was so angry with him that it wasn't until I was nearly home that I spared a thought for Luis.' She began to sob.

Wisely, Melanie let her cry for a few moments and then said bracingly, 'Come on, drink up your tea while it's hot.'

Sniffing, Alexia smiled weakly at her friend, and sipped some of the hot liquid.

'Look, love,' said Melanie, 'it's right that you should mourn Luis. He was a sweet, kind man, and you were married to him for four years. But it was a marriage of convenience—a working partnership— wasn't it? I mean, looking after him and Juan when your sister died. You know, I still think it was wrong of your Uncle Walter to insist on you marrying Luis. You could just as easily have moved in, and looked after him and the baby.'

'Uncle Walter was, and is, such a stickler for all the proprieties being observed. He was shocked beyond measure when Antonia insisted on having the baby before marrying Luis. If she hadn't died . . . well, it would have been a different story. As it was . . .'

'As it was,' Melanie said firmly, 'you married, in name only, a dying man and took on your sister's baby.' She regarded the girl fondly. 'I know it hasn't been easy, love, and you've worked your fingers to the bone for them both.'

'I don't regret it, you know. I'd do it again tomorrow, if I had to,' Alexia said with determination.

'Yes, I know you would. Still, those days are behind you now—let's give three cheers for the computer in the basement! By the way, one of your outworkers left a parcel for you, it's in the hall.'

'Good. I don't want to get behind with the order from my new software distributor. That reminds me, I've got to work on the CPU tonight . . .'

'Hold it!' Melanie shook her head in mock dismay. 'Remember me? I'm the one who doesn't know a computer when she sees one! It's all double-dutch, love.'

'Sorry,' Alexia smiled, 'I get carried away sometimes.'

'Don't be sorry! Those monsters in the basement provided Luis with all the comfort and nursing home care that money could buy. You have every right to be proud of your success. How's the business going?'

'Fine—touch wood! The real money in computers is in the royalties—the copyright on the programmes I print and put on to the disks. The royalties are really starting to roll in now, and this looks like being a good year.'

'Fantastic!' Melanie raised her cup. 'Here's to your continued success. Now,' she said, pouring them each another cup of tea, 'tell me all about Luis's brother.'

'Well, I've told you all I know. The man's impossible!' Alexia shrugged. 'Something odd, though. He said Luis had a mother and sister in Madrid.'

'Good gracious!' Melanie whistled in surprise. 'I wonder why Luis never mentioned them. He didn't, did he?'

Alexia looked puzzled. 'No, never. I can't understand why not. Mind you, if they're anything like his brother, maybe he had a point!'

'He can't be that bad, surely? What's his name—the brother, I mean?'

Alexia frowned. 'I can't remember. He did give me a card—I think I put it in my handbag . . . yes, here it is.' She handed the visiting card to Melanie, who stared at it perplexed.

'You know,' she said slowly, 'I've seen that name recently. It's ringing a terrific bell, but I can't quite place it. Maddening, I'm sure I know . . .' she drummed her fingers on the table in exasperation. 'What's he look like?'

'I don't really remember, I was so angry with him.' Alexia concentrated. 'Let's see; he's tall and very tanned—Spanish, of course—but speaks very good English. That's about all really . . .' She laughed, as Melanie raised her eyes to the ceiling in mock exasperation. 'O.K., O.K., I'm trying! He's youngish, about thirty, I should think. Dark, sort of hooded eyes, high cheekbones, with longish wavy hair that touches his collar, and . . . and a very straight nose for looking down at lesser mortals!' She sighed. 'That's it—I told you I couldn't remember much because . . .'

'*Rafael Valverde*—of course!' Melanie shrieked. 'How silly of me not to have connected his name with Luis before now. Well, fancy that!'

Alexia shrugged. 'His name doesn't mean anything to me.'

'Rafael Valverde—you know, the singer.'

Alexia looked blankly at her friend. 'It's no good, Melanie. I've never heard of him.'

'You must have!' Melanie was bouncing up and down in her chair. 'His record, "Give Me Your love" is top of the hit parade at the moment. My girls are mad about him, and so, for that matter, is Harold's mother. Do you know, she actually went out and bought tickets for one of his concerts at the Albert Hall this week. She's going with two of her friends, and none of them are a day under sixty!'

Alexia shrugged and sipped her tea. 'He may be great on the stage, but he's a nasty piece of work in real life, I can tell you.'

'Great? Don't be silly—he's fantastic! And when he smiles—wow!' Melanie stared at the girl in puzzlement. 'You must have seen him on TV—he's going to be on "Top of the Pops" this evening.' She sighed and looked dreamily into space. 'He makes even my middle-aged heart skip a beat, I can tell you! Are you sure you haven't heard of him?'

'Melanie dear, cross my heart I haven't.' Alexia laughed. 'The pop scene isn't really my thing. Especially when as soon as Juan's gone to bed I go downstairs and work. It doesn't leave much time for watching TV, you know,' she added gently.

'Yes, I do know, and it's a crying shame that for a girl of twenty-three, you've had no life to speak of. You ought to be out having fun. A beauty like you, cooped up with your computer . . .'

'Beauty? Hah! Technically speaking, by the way, it's a micro-computer!'

'Well, you should spare a moment from your micro-what's-it and really *look* at yourself. You're a truly beautiful girl, and it's all going to waste. I can't bear it!'

Alexia giggled, and pulled a face at her friend. 'I see myself at least once a day in the mirror, and it doesn't strike me as anything to write home about. Besides, I love my work, I really do. I suppose I'm just a career woman at heart.' She stood up. 'Come on, I'm going to pour us both a drink, if Harold won't feel I'm leading you from the path of wifely virtue, that is!'

'I'd love one, thanks.' Melanie smiled at the girl. I'm right, she thought, as she followed her into the sitting room. Alexia's long, thick gold hair was loosely piled up in a knot on top of her head, small tendrils of hair escaping to frame her face with soft curls. Her warm creamy skin glowed with health, setting off her large, brilliant green eyes.

'I wish I looked like you,' Melanie mused. 'I'd leave Harold and float off to the South of France, where a millionaire with a yacht would sweep me off my feet . . .'

'That's a "washing-up-at-the-sink" dream,' laughed Alexia. 'You'd be bored to sobs without Harold and the children.'

'Maybe,' agreed Melanie, 'but I'm willing to give it a try!'

'Poor Luis,' said Alexia, crestfallen. 'Here we are, laughing, and . . .'

'I'm going to sound hard,' her friend spoke firmly, 'but you must concentrate on keeping cheerful—for Juan's sake. He really needs you now—you're all he's got. Luis has had a merciful release from all his pain, and he would be the last person to want you to grieve for him. I know you were fond of him, but you must make your own life now.'

Sighing, Alexia nodded. Melanie was right, her duty was to the living, and that meant Juan. Horrified, she glanced at her watch.

'Heavens, we've been gossiping here, and I nearly forgot to say goodnight to Juan! Make yourself comfortable, I'll just run upstairs and tuck him in. I won't be a moment.'

Coming downstairs some time later, she found Melanie had switched the TV on and was watching the beginning of 'Top of the Pops'.

'Isn't he awful?' Alexia groaned, as the compère for the show went into his opening patter.

'Hush! Quick—sit down.' Melanie waved a hand at her. 'Your Rafael's going to be on in a moment.'

'He's certainly not *my* Rafael, thank you very

much!' Alexia muttered, as nevertheless she obeyed her friend, and sat down in front of the TV set.

'. . . and now, guys and gals—someone who's Famous in France, Big in Brazil, Great in Germany and a Smash in the States! Yes, folks—all the way from Sunny Spain—*Rafael Valverde!*'

'Ugh, what an introduction!' groaned Alexia as the picture dissolved to focus on the man she had met at the cemetery. He sat perched on a stool, one foot touching the floor as he began to sing a soft haunting melody. Reluctantly, despite her dislike of the man, Alexia found herself relaxing as his warm voice caressed the notes, sending shivers down her back. His charm was obvious, his smile infectious, and it wasn't until he had finished his song, to a storm of applause, that she blinked back to life. It took Melanie a little longer to return to reality.

'Isn't he gorgeous?' she breathed, her eyes glazed.

'Come on, Melanie!' Alexia gave a nervous laugh. 'He's got charisma all right, I'll grant you that. He may be fabulous on TV or on the stage, but he's not at all like that in real life. I promise you he's not.'

'You must have said something to upset him.'

'I didn't have a chance to say a damn thing—or hardly anything. I give you my word, he was furiously angry before he even met me, and I've no idea why. For instance, he practically threw Luis's will at me . . . Oh, my goodness! I'd completely forgotten . . .' She jumped up and went into the kitchen, rummaging in her handbag.

'Here we are,' she said, coming back into the room. 'He gave me this envelope which he said contained Luis's will—as if Luis had anything to leave anyone, poor man—and commanded me to present myself at his hotel tomorrow, at six sharp. He didn't even tell me which hotel. He's so arrogant, you simply wouldn't believe it!'

'Let's see,' Melanie took the envelope from Alexia's hands. 'Well, it's addressed to him at Claridges, so it's a safe bet that's where he's staying.' She handed the envelope back to the girl. 'Well, go on—open it.'

Alexia began to read, the blood draining from her face, leaving it pale and ashen. '*Oh no!* Luis can't have done this—he can't have done this to me! He must have known what his brother was like. Oh no!'

'For God's sake, what is it?' demanded Melanie.

'Read it yourself,' Alexia said dully, collapsing on to a chair, as the older woman perused the legal jargon.

'Well, it's not too bad, Alexia. I see he's made Rafael the boy's legal guardian.'

'Read on,' groaned the girl.

'Oh,' Melanie paused. 'Yes, I see. That bit about wishing his son to be brought up in Spain and learning to be a Spaniard?'

'Bingo!' said Alexia. 'Can you see the oh-so-charming Rafael, who appears for some reason to hate my guts, allowing Juan to remain here with me? I wouldn't put any money on it if I were you.'

'There's a simple answer, Alexia—you can take the matter to court, surely?'

'I suppose I can try, except they're bound to take into account Luis's last wishes, aren't they? I mean, I'm only an aunt after all, and there seem to be lots of relatives in Spain.'

'Well, you can't do anything tonight. Why not sleep on it and see your Uncle Walter in the morning? He is a solicitor, isn't he? He'll know what to do.'

'Oh God, I hope so—I really hope so!'

CHAPTER TWO

ALEXIA hesitated outside the door of Rafael Valverde's hotel suite, trying to summon up her courage for the forthcoming confrontation. Her Uncle Walter had been very explicit when she had seen him that morning.

'Unless both you and Luis's brother can amicably agree on Juan's future, it will have to be resolved in court.'

Alexia looked at him with a worried frown. 'If we have to go to court, what will happen then?'

Her uncle lay back in his large leather chair, his thin lips pursed as he gazed at the ceiling. 'Let me see,' he placed his hands together, looking pensive. 'It will depend very much on whether the court believes you to be a fit person, morally and financially, to look after Juan. The other factor would be his dead father's wishes . . .'

'What you're saying,' she interrupted sharply, 'is that it could go either way?'

'Precisely, my dear.' Her uncle beamed at her. 'You see, it's an interesting little problem. On the one hand we have a devoted aunt, who has supported her . . . er . . . husband and nephew for the last four years. There's no doubt you looked after them very well, my dear Alexia, no doubt at all. I'm very proud of you.' He paused to study Luis's will. 'On the other hand, your late husband has left no doubt in this document that he wishes his son to be brought up in Spain, and has granted the guardianship of his son to his brother. Uncle versus aunt—very interesting!'

Alexia sighed with despondency. 'I can't understand why Luis should have done this to me, and why he never mentioned his family in Spain. It all seems so unfair!'

'My dear, he was undoubtedly making the best provision he could for his son. Maybe he felt you'd carried his burdens far enough?'

'It wasn't much of a burden, Uncle, and . . . and . . . Juan is Antonia's son. I did promise her if anything happened . . .'

'Yes, yes,' Walter Harrison interjected fussily, his pale cheeks tinged with pink. 'Well, we really don't want to discuss your sister's . . . er . . . carryings on. I made myself very clear on that subject a long time ago. Thank God your father and mother were dead. That a niece of mine should . . . Well, it's all in the past, Alexia. We are now dealing with the present, and indeed the future.'

He gazed down at the paper in front of him. 'I very strongly urge you to come to some sort of arrangement with this . . . er . . . this Rafael Valverde. The courts will decide solely on what is best for Juan, and you should do the same. That's it, my dear,' he said, getting up to open his door and show her out. 'That's it. Concentrate on Juan's interests, and don't deny him his heritage.'

It's all very well for Uncle Walter to tell me to concentrate on Juan's interests, thought Alexia, knocking on the door of Rafael's suite. He hasn't got to deal with Luis's fierce brother, and I wish to heaven that I didn't have to, either.

The door was opened by a short, fat, balding man, wearing a brightly striped jacket. 'You got an appointment?' he demanded in a strong American accent.

'Why—yes, I think so. This is Rafael Valverde's suite, isn't it?'

'Sure is, but I warn you, I've thrown out six girls already this afternoon. I've had you autograph-hunters up to here!' The fat American tapped the top of his bald head.

Alexia looked at him in astonishment. 'I can assure you that I have no intention of asking for Mr Valverde's autograph. I'm here,' she took a deep breath, 'I'm simply here to see him, and by appointment. He ... er ... it appears that he's my brother-in-law, and ...'

'Sure, sure. Rafael did say something about you calling by today. Come on in, honey,' he said, issuing her into a splendidly decorated sitting room. 'I wonder why old Rafael didn't say anything about what a lovely-looking gal you are? Downright sneaky of him, don't you think?' He smiled broadly with frank admiration at Alexia. 'Yes, siree! You're one hell of a good-looking dame. Ever been on the stage?'

Alexia, feeling stunned by the rapid fire of the American's speech, could only manage to stutter, '... Er ... no ... I haven't, Mr ... er ...'

'It's Henry Zeiss, honey, at your service any time. I'm old Rafael's agent—in America, that is. Just over here for a flying visit. The boy's got a big venue at Madison Square Garden in two weeks' time, and we're just tying up some loose ends.'

Alexia looked around the large, empty room. 'If Mr Valverde isn't here, I can come back later.' She suddenly felt nervous, wishing herself a million miles away.

'No sweat, honey. He's here. He's just finishing an interview with a couple of lovely lady journalists. Through there, in the bedroom!' he added, with a leer.

'Well, in that case I wouldn't dream of disturbing him.' Alexia turned to leave. If this was 'show business', she thought with distaste, then she was heartily glad she had not encountered it before now.

'Now, honey, there's no need to rush off. He'll be through in a moment. Here, let me take your coat.' She hesitated for a moment and then shrugged helplessly, allowing him to help her out of the garment.

Alexia had dressed with particular care before coming to see Rafael, anxious to look as old and responsible as possible. She had finally chosen a simple, soft black wool dress with a high polo-necked collar, plain fitted bodice and softly gathered skirt. She had thought she looked businesslike, and was therefore startled by Henry Zeiss's view of her ensemble, as he stood back looking at the slim girl in front of him.

'Ver-ry nice! I bet you'd strip to advantage, honey.'

'Really, Mr Zeiss! I ...' This visit to Rafael's hotel wasn't going at all the way she had thought it would. She tried to freeze the impertinent man with an icy look, which seemed to have absolutely no affect.

'I've got an interest in some strip-joints back home. You want a job any time, let me know. You know what you remind me of, honey? One of those broads in the Moulin Rouge. You know, the gals painted by that bearded guy with no legs.'

Feeling somewhat lightheaded by the direction the day seemed to be taking, Alexia was unable to repress a gurgle of laughter, 'Do you mean Toulouse-Lautrec?'

'That's the one, honey. Your hair's styled just right for one of his paintings. Jeez, that guy was lucky! No legs, and he still got the girls!' He roared with laughter, both at his own joke and Alexia's astonished expression, which gave way to a wide grin as she began to giggle helplessly.

The connecting door to Rafael's bedroom opened at that moment, as he issued two women out before him. The elder of the two, a woman in her early forties, turned and gushingly thanked Rafael, somewhat pink in the face as she nervously patted her hair. The other journalist, much younger and prettier Alexia noticed, just stood gazing adoringly at the Spaniard. He gave them both a beaming smile lifting the younger woman's hand to his lips as he led them towards the door.

'Goodbye, ladies. It has been a great pleasure—a great pleasure indeed,' he purred smoothly as they left the suite.

Ugh! How smarmy can you get? thought Alexia in disgust.

'Rafael baby, I've got to hand it to you. You obviously had that tough old bag eating right out of your hand!' The agent laughed and turned to Alexia. 'He's a wonder with the women . . . he really is!'

'I'm sure he is!' Alexia's voice was scathing, her eyes raked Rafael's tall figure with contempt.

'It is work,' Rafael shrugged dismissively as he regarded Alexia from beneath his dark brows with grim censure. 'You are late,' he added sternly. 'Even in the bedroom I could hear you both laughing. I am surprised that you should be capable of such amusement, so soon after your husband's death.'

'You are also late,' she flashed back, 'and how I mourn Luis is my own business!'

'Oh-oh! I think this is definitely a case of unfriendly relations. It's time I left, Rafael, I'll see you tomorrow.' Henry Zeiss turned to Alexia. 'It's been a real pleasure, honey.'

His departure gave them both some time to collect themselves, before Rafael broke the silence. 'Would you care for a drink?'

'Yes, please,' she said, mortified that she should have been caught on the raw so early in their meeting. Luis's brother seemed to have an almost uncanny knack of making her say and do the wrong things.

Rafael went over to a small bar in the corner of the room to pour her drink, and Alexia took the opportunity to study the man who was beginning to feature so largely in her life.

There was no doubt at all that he was startlingly good-looking, dressed in a pair of tight dark trousers that gripped his slim hips, his open-necked white shirt, made of raw silk and tailored to emphasise both his slim waist and broad shoulders, contrasting sharply with his tanned complexion. Alexia coloured slightly as he handed her a glass, before he went over to sit down in a chair on the other side of the room.

'Aren't you having something to drink too?' she asked in surprise.

'No, thank you. I have to work later this evening, and I never drink before a performance if I can help it.'

He sat regarding her in silence from beneath his hooded eyes, and nervously Alexia tried to make conversation. 'I . . . er . . . I believe you're a singer.'

'Yes, I do sing. Surely you knew that?' he replied in a bored, patient voice, as if talking to a child.

'No, of course I didn't know. How could I, when I didn't know of your existence until yesterday?' she retorted crossly. Really, the vanity of the man was insufferable!

'Ah yes,' he shrugged. 'Luis's estrangement from his family was regrettable and a matter of great sorrow, especially to his mother.'

'I'm sure it was.' Alexia suddenly felt acutely sorry for the woman who had lost her son. 'But what I can't understand is why you never wrote to him, even if he didn't write to you?'

'Simply because we had no idea of his address. I knew, of course, that he was somewhere in the London area, but he was not listed in the telephone book. It never occurred to us that it would be entered under your maiden name of Harrison,' he added grimly.

'For business reasons I . . .'

'Since I learnt of your address two days ago,' he went on as though she hadn't spoken, 'I have had some enquiries made. I understand that you live in a house in South Kensington, in some comfort,' he sneered. 'I am surprised that Luis was able to afford to live in such a style.'

Alexia wasn't sure she could take much more of this man's rudeness. Controlling herself with difficulty, she said abruptly, 'No, he wasn't able to afford it.'

'So you paid for everything?' he queried with a sceptical glance at the slim girl sitting opposite him.

'If it's any business of yours—which it certainly isn't—yes, I did "pay for everything", as you so elegantly put it!'

'I can think of another way to put it,' he said in a voice dripping with contempt, 'but I am not used to using such words in front of a woman!'

Alexia gasped. 'I don't know if you're deliberately trying to be offensive, but you're certainly succeeding, *señor*!' She was appalled to hear her voice raised in anger. Why, her behaviour was becoming as bad as his! She couldn't understand the strange effect he had on her, but she knew she had never met anyone who could arouse, so quickly, such primitive feelings of fury within her.

Sipping her drink, she took a deep breath and attempted to explain her position to Rafael, as calmly as she could.

'You must understand that Luis was very ill, for a long time—the last four years, in fact. Do please be reasonable. Someone had to earn the money, and he just wasn't able to. I'm not ashamed of working. Why on earth should I be?'

'And Luis approved of such behaviour? I can hardly believe that!' he laughed scornfully.

'You can damn well believe what you like. "Such behaviour", indeed!' Abandoning all control, Alexia jumped to her feet, shaking with rage. 'Don't try to tell me that no woman in Spain goes out to work, even when she's married, because I refuse to believe it!'

Rafael, becoming as angry as Alexia, rose and walked towards her. 'Yes,' he hissed, 'women do work in Spain, but no decent woman would do what you have done.'

'*What have I done?* You're mad—stark, raving mad!' she cried, suddenly breathless at his proximity, his dark eyes burning fiercely down into hers. She backed away from his lean, powerful figure, confused by the sparks of tension which crackled between them. 'At least,' she cried recklessly, goaded beyond reason, 'at least I don't ponce about on a stage, and . . . and sing sloppy love songs!'

'*Bastante! Silencio!*' He grasped her by the shoulders and shook her roughly. 'That is enough . . . do you understand?'

Shaken and confused by his violence and her own reactions, Alexia stumbled and fell forward against his chest. She gasped and raised her face to his. Rafael

looked down into the large green, gold-flecked eyes
and trembling mouth of the startled girl . . .

His arms tightened about her while time seemed to
stand still for a moment, as they gazed mesmerised at
each other. His firm lips slowly descended to take
possession of hers, and instinctively she struggled to
escape. Ignoring her puny efforts, his mouth began to
invade hers with a ruthlessly savage kiss, the like of
which she had never known.

Her senses began to swim, helpless as the burning
pressure of his mouth ignited a flame within her.
Without conscious thought she innocently and yet
instinctively arched her body closer to his, moaning
softly as his kiss deepened.

Rafael abruptly withdrew his mouth, swearing
savagely under his breath as he pushed her roughly
from him, before walking over to stand looking out of
the window. Shaken and trembling, Alexia stood with
a hand pressed against her bruised lips.

'You—you behave like an animal!' she cried, weak
with shock. Her mouth was burning, her body
trembling and aching with an unfamiliar pain.

'*Por Dios!* It is surely from "animals" like myself
that you derive your living,' he commented bleakly,
still looking out of the window.

'*What!*' Her thoughts in a whirl, Alexia sank slowly
down into an armchair, trying to stop her limbs from
trembling. He couldn't think . . . surely not . . .? But if
he did, it would explain many things she had not
understood. She must try and make a supreme effort
and ignore what had happened . . . somehow. She had
to try and attempt to rescue this interview . . . for
Juan's sake . . .

'Rafael,' she said, her face still flushed, 'will you . . .
will you please come and sit down, and tell me,

plainly, exactly how you think I . . . I earn my living?'

He walked over to a chair, and sat down, his face a blank mask. 'I don't think—I know. Luis was very explicit the last time I talked to him. I had a singing engagement here in London, and we met for dinner afterwards. He told me he had fallen in love with a girl, and that she was expecting a baby. Unfortunately this girl, a Miss A. Harrison, I remember the name quite clearly, had been a high-class call girl.' He brushed a hand distractedly through his dark wavy hair.

'He didn't blame her, as I would have done—and do!' he added contemptuously. 'He wasn't even sure the child was his and, what is more, he didn't seem to care. *Es increíble! no?* Poor Luis, he even tried to excuse her behaviour by explaining that she had no training for a career—no other way of earning her living. *Dios!*'

He rose and began to pace about the room. 'So perhaps you will tell me, Señora Luis Valverde,' he turned to stare fixedly at Alexia, 'just how do you earn your living nowadays?'

My God! she thought, her mind in a chaotic whirl. He thinks I'm Antonia! And that means he must believe that I'm Juan's mother, not his aunt. She tried to weigh up the pros and cons of telling Rafael the truth. Even if she did, he wasn't likely to believe her, but for her own self-respect she had to try. However, on the other hand, if he believed Juan was her child, it would mean that he was more likely to concede her right to bring the little boy up here in Britain. Still . . .

'I run a computer business,' she said quietly, trying to control her nervously trembling hands.

'Hah! I have heard of computer dating, but I did not know that it included going that far! *Por Dios!*, I need a drink,' he muttered, striding over to pour himself a neat whisky.

Alexia smiled weakly. 'Come on, Rafael. You can't seriously imagine that I can afford a large London house, an au pair and all Luis's medical expenses by . . . by entertaining gentlemen! Have some sense . . .' She laughed wryly at the whole concept which was so absurd.

'I only wish that it had been that easy, but alas it wasn't,' she continued. 'Put succinctly, I and the girls I employ, produce programs and floppy disks for computer software distributors. Despite some tight moments in the early days I'm now doing very well, having cornered a nice little market in stock control programmes.'

'I do not understand this "floppy disk" you talk about, and I neither know nor care what you do now,' he snarled arrogantly. 'However, I know *what you were*, and that is quite enough for me!' He sank back in his chair, sipping his drink, his expression hard and grim.

Alexia's green eyes flashed with fury. Bloody man! How dared he dismiss all her hard work with such contempt! She was shocked and dismayed, used as she was to a peaceful, ordered existence, to discover that she was capable of such a fiery dislike of the man before her. He seemed determined to believe that she was Antonia—and short of dragging Uncle Walter halfway across London, there did not seem to be any way she could prove she was not. Besides, Antonia had had enough mud slung at her while she was alive, what right had this man to judge her now she was dead?

Dear, silly, feather-brained Antonia was dead, and there was no way she was going to let this supercilious Spaniard pour any more of his vitriol on her memory. If he wanted to think Alexia was Antonia—so be it.

She stood up. 'I came here to discuss Luis's will, but there seems little point in doing so. I was hoping, for Juan's sake, that we could come to an amicable arrangement. It would seem that such a thought was laughable.'

'The boy is half Spanish. He should meet his family and know his native country.' Rafael looked sternly at the slim girl as she reached for her handbag, preparing to depart. 'You must see the justice of what I say?'

'What I see,' she snapped, 'is blind prejudice and your inability—or stupidity—in not being able to hear the truth when you hear it!'

He rose and walked over to put his empty glass on the mantelpiece. 'His father appointed me to be his guardian, and I intend to see that his wishes are complied with,' he said firmly.

'You're making a great start, I must say! Trying . . . trying to tear Juan away from me! I promise you, I'll fight all the way, in every court in the land, and . . . and abroad if need be!' Just looking at the casually lounging figure, gazing down his arrogant nose at her, made her tremble with rage. Never before in her life had she met anyone she had hated so much.

'Oh, for heaven's sake, Alexia!' Rafael gestured wearily. 'There is no need for all this drama. I have never suggested that I wished to take your son away from you. That would indeed be cruel. I had merely wished to propose a holiday in Spain, so that Juan could meet his grandmother. Is that so strange a request?'

Alexia bit her lip with frustration. Somehow he had managed to put her in the wrong again. She simply didn't seem to be able to cope with this man.

Normally in her business dealings she was cool, calm and collected. Never had she felt so upset and unsettled as she did now. Rafael seemed to have a violently disruptive effect on her, which she did not understand.

'Juan is too young to travel on his own. Maybe we can talk about this in a few years' time,' she countered.

'*Dios!* You called me stupid just now, but it is you who are stupid! I certainly would not expect a small boy to travel alone. I assumed that you would accompany him, of course.'

'Well . . .' she said slowly, calming herself down with difficulty, 'I don't understand why you didn't issue this invitation in the first place, instead of insulting me and . . . and calling me a . . . a loose woman!'

'I am sorry if I . . .' Rafael ran his hand distractedly through his hair. 'Come, we must have some measure of understanding between us, for Juan's sake,' he sighed with exasperation. 'Is it possible for you to bring him to Spain for a holiday?'

She shrugged her shoulders with a marked lack of enthusiasm. 'Yes, I suppose so. When?'

He went over to his jacket which was hanging on a chair. He extracted a diary, and checked it swiftly. 'It is now the middle of May. I will be free from the twentieth of June, for a month. My family will be at our holiday home on the Costa del Sol, so Juan will be able to swim and build sand castles. He would like that?' He suddenly smiled at Alexia. 'I know I would have done at his age.'

'He would love it,' she smiled faintly and warily back at the tall Spaniard. 'I'm not sure I can take a whole month off from work, but I'll try to arrange it.'

'*Esta muy bien.* Good, that's settled, then.' He

breathed a sigh of relief. Having to deal with this very beautiful, but also very difficult Englishwoman, was proving to be exhausting.

'Er ... Rafael ...' Alexia hesitated, 'I ... er ... at the risk of making you angry again, may I please point out that there have been some cases of parents or guardians trying to keep children in a country, when such holidays have ended? I would require a legal guarantee from you before I leave this country.'

'Of course, if you wish,' he said stiffly, 'but I would give you my word.'

Alexia gave a mirthless laugh. 'Quite useless in law, I'm afraid. In my business I concentrate on reading the small print in contracts. Not by trusting to fate and "entertaining" gentlemen, as you so fondly imagine!'

Rafael ground his teeth in fury as he went off to collect her coat. She knew it was a petty triumph, but she grinned as she heard him mutter what she was sure were violent Spanish oaths, before he returned.

'I can put it on myself,' she said hurriedly, practically snatching the coat from his hands. She had absolutely no intention of letting him near her again. The thought of his savage kiss made her blush and she tried to cover up her confusion. 'I ... I've been wondering how you heard about Luis's death.'

'He left instructions with his doctor to telephone my London solicitor immediately he died, with the date, time and place of his funeral. The solicitor cabled my home in Madrid, and they gave him my address in London. All very simple, no?'

He hesitated, and took a deep breath. 'I realise that I may have been rude ... unkind. I ... er ... I apologise.'

Alexia looked at him. Proud, arrogant Rafael,

actually saying he was sorry? She repressed a malicious grin, as with a bland face she said, 'Thank you, Rafael. I accept your apology. I'm afraid I can't say it's been a pleasure, because frankly it hasn't. Goodbye.'

As if he could read her mind, a gleam sparked in his dark, hooded eyes. 'Oh, there is just one more thing, Alexia.'

'Yes?' she turned to face him as he opened the door.

'I just wanted to say that I do not apologise for that delightful kiss. Oh no, not at all! I enjoyed it immensely.' He gave her a brilliant smile, roaring with laughter as she blushed a deep crimson.

'You . . . you . . . male chauvinist pig!' she hissed, and turned away to stalk down the carpeted corridor, the peals of his laughter ringing about her ears.

CHAPTER THREE

IT was only ten in the morning, but already the sun was high in the Spanish sky. Alexia rolled over on the sunbed so that she could keep an eye on Juan and his friends in the paddling pool. There was really no need for her to bother, she thought wryly. Rosa, Luis's old nanny, had gathered Juan to her bosom the moment they had arrived. He was in a fair way to becoming spoilt, as his grandmother and most of the household staff competed for his favours. She watched the children splashing each other with shrieks of delight, under the watchful eye of Rosa who sat knitting in the shade of an old fig tree.

Glancing down at her body, already turning a golden brown, she blushed slightly. Before this trip to Spain she had never worn a bikini and she still wasn't used to the display of so much of her flesh. However, Melanie had been very forthright when Alexia had shown her the clothes she proposed to take on holiday.

'You can throw most of these away immediately! Honestly, Alexia, you've got bags of money to spend now, and these dowdy "sensible" dresses are only fit for the local jumble sale. As for this,' she held up a blue bathing suit with thick straps, 'where in the world did you get it?'

'Do you mind! That's my old school swimming costume.'

'Yes, I do mind. It's a real passion-killer if ever I saw one!' laughed Melanie. 'I'll tell you what—as soon as I've taken the girls to school tomorrow morning, we'll go shopping, and see if we can't get you properly equipped for a holiday in the sun.'

'I can't spare the time,' Alexia said regretfully. 'There's so much to do and ...'

'Oh yes, you can,' her friend said firmly. 'If you're planning to be away for a month, you'll have to learn to delegate some of your work anyway. It seems to me that you may as well start now.'

'O.K., O.K. ... you win!' Alexia grinned. 'Now stop nagging.'

As promised, Melanie collected her the next morning and they spent most of the day in and out of the big stores in Oxford Street, arriving home tired and weary, late in the afternoon.

'Put the kettle on, there's a love,' Melanie groaned as she brought in the last of the carrier-bags and boxes from the car. 'Oh-h, that's better!' Sighing with relief, she slipped off her shoes. 'Why is it that shopping is so exhausting? Mind you,' she added, 'there's nothing nicer than helping to spend someone else's money.' She surveyed with satisfaction the large pile of parcels.

'I don't know how you talked me into all this extravagance,' sighed Alexia. 'I've never spent so much money on clothes in my whole life. I feel positively wicked! Of course,' she added hurriedly, 'I'm very grateful for all your help, but ... well, I'm still not very happy about those bikinis. They're ... well, they're so rude ...'

'Nonsense! You've earned the money, why shouldn't you spend some of it on yourself? As for those bikinis, all I can say is that you should go to the South of France. Harold and I went to Cannes for a week last year, and most of the girls on the beach were topless!'

'Well, if anyone expects me to expose my all in Spain, they can think again!' Alexia retorted indignantly.

'Oh, for heaven's sake, relax. No one suggested anything of the sort.' Melanie sipped her tea. 'You know,' she continued, 'you've been like a cat on hot bricks since your meeting with Rafael Valverde. I can't think why you're so upset. All he wanted was to give Juan a chance to meet his Spanish relatives—nothing strange about that, surely?'

'Put that way, it all sounds very reasonable. But . . .' Alexia shook her head distractedly, 'he's the most unreasonable man I've ever met. He's insulting and rude and . . .' she blushed as she recalled the strength of his arms about her, his demanding kiss, '. . . and prejudiced. My God, is he prejudiced!' she cried angrily, banging her fist on the kitchen table. 'I haven't had a chance to tell you, but he thinks that I'm Antonia, and I can't persuade him to accept that I'm not. Furthermore,' she added with some heat, 'he's convinced that I've got a big red light fixed up outside this house, and have a constant stream of male visitors to pay the household expenses!'

Melanie hooted with laughter and Alexia relaxed, grinning at her friend. 'I'm not joking. He really does think I run a house of—what's the expression?—of ill-repute.'

'Oh, come on!' her friend gasped, wiping the tears of laughter from her eyes.

'I'm not kidding! I told him I run a computer business, and do you know what his reaction was?' Alexia assumed a heavy Spanish accent, 'Ho-ho! Computer dating? I did not know that it included going that far, duckie; or words to that effect.'

By now Melanie was helpless with mirth, and even Alexia was beginning to see the funny side of her extraordinary meeting with Rafael.

'Seriously,' said Melanie, when she had stopped

laughing and was drinking a second cup of tea, 'I can see that it's possible he might well have thought you were Antonia, before he met you. After all, your maiden name and initials are the same. But he'd have to be as blind as a bat to continue making a mistake like that on a second meeting. I mean, it's so obvious.'

'Is it? Why?'

'Well, I don't want to speak ill of your sister, I never met the girl and she's dead now, poor thing. But really, dear, if there's one thing about you, it's that you simply reek of virginity.'

'Charming! Thanks very much.'

'Frankly, in this day and age, it is charming. I mean,' Melanie strove to explain, 'you've concentrated so hard on your work to the exclusion of all else that you have had little or no contact with the opposite sex, outside of business, that is. I know you can cope with the men you meet in the computer field, and beat them at their own game. However, when you've been to some of our parties, you shy away like a startled filly at the first amorous approach; and with your looks,' she added enviously, 'you can't blame the men for trying.'

'Oh, Melanie . . . I . . .'

'It all comes back to what I said two weeks ago,' said her friend firmly. 'It's all very well having a career, and working hard at it, but you mustn't forget you're a woman too. It's not your fault that your life is out of balance at the moment, but you've got a month's holiday in front of you to relax and have fun—good, old-fashioned fun.'

'You're absolutely right, as always,' Alexia smiled, 'and it really will be marvellous to have a good rest and soak up the sun. However, I don't think there's likely to be any "fun" within Rafael's orbit . . . he'll make sure of that! Honestly, he's so full of anger and disapproval of me that I'm really dreading having to meet him again. As for living in the same house . . . let's hope it's large enough, so that I can keep well away from him.'

'Well, dear,' said Melanie, getting up to go, 'there's something not quite right about all this. He's obviously an experienced man of the world, and he must have met or seen far more shocking things than poor Antonia's fall from grace. He seems, from all you say, to be overreacting in a most extraordinary manner.' She thought for a moment. 'Unless . . . He didn't try and—well, make advances to you, did he?'

'Of course not,' Alexia lied hurriedly. There was no way she could possibly relate what had happened, even to such a good friend as Melanie.

'Never mind, maybe he'll have calmed down by the time you arrive in Spain. Now I must go and leave you to unpack all those lovely clothes!'

The flight to Malaga had been uneventful, and Juan had enjoyed himself asking a hundred and one questions about the aeroplane, before falling asleep for the last hour of the journey. Alexia was glad of the silence, since she was both mentally and physically exhausted by the amount of work she had had to do before leaving. Her main client, who had become a good friend over the years, had given her a large order which she was loath to turn down. Luckily, he had agreed to accept half the work before, and the rest after she had returned from her holiday.

'It looks as if we're both going to Spain,' he had said, at their last meeting. 'Where are you staying?'

'I don't really know, Michael. It's somewhere with an unpronounceable name, near Marbella, I think.'

'Great! I'm staying with friends at the Marbella Club. Give me a ring when you're settled in, and we can meet for a drink and a meal.'

'I'd love that.' Alexia was relieved to think that she would at least know someone in Spain. It was a comforting thought with which to face a journey into the unknown.

They had landed at Malaga mid-afternoon. Progressing swiftly through Customs, they came out into the main hall of the airport, blinking in the strong sunshine.

'Señora Valverde?' A smartly dressed man in black trousers, white shirt and black tie bowed before her.

'Yes . . . I, mean *si*,' she said, smiling both at the man and at her first attempt at the Spanish language. As Juan had been the only child on the flight, she supposed their identification had been a simple matter.

'Please to come, *señora*,' said the man, picking up her cases and leading the way through the glass doors towards a large black car, with what seemed to be a policeman in a greeny-grey uniform standing by it, talking to someone inside the vehicle.

As they approached, a tall man in dark glasses opened the rear door and got out to walk towards them.

'Welcome to Spain, Alexia,' smiled Rafael, removing his glasses, before squatting down with bent knees to greet the small boy. 'You must be Juan. I am very pleased to meet you at last.'

Juan smiled back, hopping up and down with excitement. 'Hello, Uncle Rafael. Do you know, I've been in a big aeroplane! It was super!'

'Yes, I know.' Laughing, Rafael rose and picked the boy up in his arms. 'Now we are going for a drive in my car and you will see the sea.'

'Can I swim today? I want to learn to swim straight away. Can you swim? Alexia says the Mediterranean Sea has no tide. Is that really true?'

'Absolutely true,' said Rafael, ruffling the boy's hair. 'You are a very clever boy for your age, but that is enough questions for the moment.'

Alexia stood looking on in surprise—not only that Rafael should have bothered to come and meet them himself, but also at his friendly reception and kindness to Juan. He didn't seem to be the same man she had met in London.

She was so immersed in her thoughts that it was a moment or two before she noticed the increasing noise around them. She looked up to see people, mostly women, shouting to each other and pointing excitedly in the direction of their car. Rafael swore, and spoke rapidly in Spanish to both their driver and the policeman, who immediately whistled for reinforcements.

'*Vamos—pronto!* Into the car as quickly as you can,' Rafael commanded, hurriedly putting Juan on to the back seat before pushing Alexia inside and swiftly following her, only managing to slam the car door shut in the nick of time. She looked out of the window to see a crowd of people yelling, 'Raf-a-el ... Raf-a-el!' pressing their faces to the windows and brandishing pieces of paper, before her view was obscured by the broad backs of policemen surrounding the vehicle.

The chauffeur moved the car slowly forward, although one or two women managed to break through the police cordon to bang on the roof and windows. Their vehicle gathered speed and Rafael leant back in the seat beside her, sighing heavily.

'What was going on back there?' She turned to him

with startled eyes. 'It was ... well, it was quite frightening for a moment.'

'I'm sorry. It is part of what you might call the penalty of fame,' he shrugged, smiling reassuringly at her and Juan. 'I realised that there might be a risk of being recognised, which is why I waited in the car until you arrived.'

'You mean,' she said, realisation slowly dawning, 'it's because you sing? All those people going mad out there, treating you like a pop star ...'

He laughed. 'My dear Alexia, I *am* a pop star. I regret to tell you that I really do "ponce about on the stage singing sloppy love songs" as you so frankly put it!'

'Oh! I—I ...' she shrank back against the seat of the car, blushing deeply, staring down at her hands and trying not to look at him, as she recalled her angry words in the hotel room. How unfair of Rafael to repeat something she had said in the heat of the moment! Not that she hadn't meant it, because she had! He really was a hateful man, and this holiday was going to be just as awful as she had feared.

'Look!' Juan shouted. 'Look, Alexia—the sea!'

Glad of the interruption, she looked out of the car window. The road seemed to hug the coast, which was a mixture of golden sandy beaches and wild rocky coves. Juan chatted away to the driver, whose lack of any real English didn't seem to disturb either of them, while Alexia sat in silence stealing occasional glances through her eyelashes at Rafael, who was gazing studiously out of the window.

He was dressed in a pair of beige linen trousers topped by a pale blue short-sleeved shirt, open at the neck. A heavy gold watch clasped the wrist of the tanned, muscular arm which lay so close to her, and she shivered as she became disturbingly aware of his strongly powerful male presence.

'I'm sorry I ... well, I'm sorry to have said anything so rude ... about your singing, I mean. I ...'

'Not the handsomest of apologies, my dear sister-in-law, but I can see it will have to do.' Rafael turned to face her with a sardonic grin.

'It's all you're going to get!' she hissed angrily, all her feelings of antagonism towards him rising swiftly to the surface.

To her surprise he laughed softly. 'How could I have forgotten what a little spitfire you are, my dear Alexia?' he murmured, taking her hand and raising it to his lips. 'You remind me of a highly bred racehorse, who needs a light hand on the bridle and a crack of the whip now and then. I shall have to see if I can't bring you under more control while you are here in Spain.'

'*You*, bring me under control? You've got a nerve!' she whispered with low venom, anxious not to draw Juan's attention to their argument as she seethed with impotent rage. Rafael's Spanish accent was more pronounced then it had been in London, the soft caressing tone of his voice, sharply at variance with his actual words, affecting her in an alarming manner.

Suddenly breathless, she inched angrily away from him, her face burning as she tried to tug away her hand which he refused to let go. To her increasing fury, he laughed gently again.

'It's no good trying to fight with me. I am determined that we shall preserve an outward show of civility, whatever our private feelings—for Juan's sake. Don't you agree that is right?'

Normally a mild-mannered girl, Alexia found herself swearing inwardly in acute frustration. The hateful man! He always managed to put her in the wrong. Of course she wouldn't do anything to upset Juan—who did he think she was . . .? She checked her thoughts suddenly. How stupid of her, she knew exactly who he thought she was . . .

'Well, is it a bargain?'

Alexia sighed. 'Yes, it's a bargain. One that I'm prepared to bet I can keep better than you,' she added bitterly, remembering some of the things he had said to her at their previous meetings.

'I accept your challenge, Alexia!' Rafael raised her hand to his lips again, before releasing it. 'Now, shall we talk of more pleasant matters?'

'Yes, of course.' She smiled grimly back at him. It would seem that, somehow, war had been declared. Well, he'd find out that two could play at that game, she thought, trying to ignore an unreasonable lump of depression in her stomach.

'Have we much further to go?' she asked.

'No, we're nearly there. This,' he gestured out of the car at the wide streets, the smart shops and pavement cafés, 'this is Marbella. My home is just a few kilometres outside the town.'

The car slowed down presently, passing through tall white gateposts, and down a winding drive flanked on either side by shrubs bearing flowers in deep pink and purple. They came to a stop outside a large white house with a wide entrance porch supported by four stone pillars.

'Here we are, Juan,' said Rafael, getting out of the car and taking the child's hand as he walked towards the entrance.

Suddenly feeling shy, Alexia hung back for a moment and then followed them slowly into the house. There seemed to be a babble of noise in the cool interior, which was dark after the brilliant sunshine outside.

Rafael turned. 'Come and meet my mother, Alexia, she has been longing to see you.'

She found herself being introduced to a small, slim, beautifully dressed woman of about fifty, with one of the kindest smiles she had ever seen. All her nervousness evaporated as the mother of Rafael and Luis clasped her in her arms, kissing her cheeks.

'*Bienvenido!* You are welcome, my child. So very welcome.' Doña Maria Valverde stood back to look at her widowed daughter-in-law. '*Que hermosa!* How beautiful you are! The little boy, he is so like Luis,' she said, turning to look at Juan surrounded by clucking and cooing women, all dressed in black, who bore him off to the kitchen.

Doña Maria laughed. 'They are going to give him some milk and biscuits, so I will show you to your room.' She led the way across the large hall, up a sweeping staircase and along a corridor to a door at the end.

Alexia's 'room' turned out to be a suite of rooms, which contained a small room for Juan, and one for a maid to sleep in if, as Doña Maria explained, Alexia should wish to go out in the evening. Her bedroom was very large, with a marble bathroom opening off it.

Alexia went to the window and found herself looking out over the sea, the house seemingly built on a promontory which jutted out from the coastline. 'It's lovely,' she breathed, turning to smile at Juan's grandmother. 'It's so kind of you to have made these arrangements for us. Thank you very much.'

'*De nada.* We will have a long talk soon, but first you will wish to wash and unpack ... yes? Why do you not have a *siesta*? We do not eat until late here in

Spain, and Rosa, Luis's old nanny, will be reluctant to let Juan go just yet.' Doña Maria laughed softly, 'I also wish to see my grandson!'

Gratefully welcoming the idea of a short nap, Alexia woke much refreshed to find Juan full of supper and ready for bed. She tucked him up and then dressed quickly for dinner. It was already almost eight o'clock—how late was 'late'?

She was also unsure of the correct dress to wear—long or short? She compromised by choosing a simple sleeveless dress of emerald silk jersey, the same colour as her eyes. Its mid-calf-length full skirt should make it acceptable, she thought, as she surveyed herself in the mirror. The soft material clung to her figure, emphasising her full breasts and slim waist, as she leant forward to clip on gold hoop earrings and to apply a coat of pale lipstick. Slipping on high-heeled gold sandals, she braced herself and left the room.

She made her way down the stairs and found the living room by following the sound of voices. Taking a deep breath, Alexia entered the room apprehensively, wishing she was back in London. The conversation stopped as the room's occupants all turned to look at her. She found the silence unnerving and wondered anxiously what was wrong, having no idea that the picture she presented, of a ravishingly lovely woman, had momentarily stunned the people present.

Doña Maria broke the heavy pause by hurrying forward to greet her. 'Come, you must meet my daughter Julia.'

Alexia immediately liked the small, plump girl of seventeen, who looked far more like Luis than Rafael. Julia smiled shyly up at the tall visitor. 'Welcome,' she said. 'I hope you enjoy your visit with us.'

'I'm sure I shall,' Alexia replied warmly. 'Your mother has been so kind.'

'I do not think you will see much of your son, if she and old Rosa have their way!' Julia laughed. 'However, I will be very happy to show you around the local shops and visit Marbella any time you like.'

Rafael's mother came up to claim Alexia and bore her off to be introduced to a beautiful slim, petite girl of about her own age, whose magnolia skin and long black curly hair would have made her outstanding in any company. Here, thought Alexia, the girl glowed like a rare jewel among mere pebbles.

'This is Isabella Sanchez—she is Rafael's fiancée. Come, Rafael,' called his mother, 'you have not yet poured Alexia a drink.'

Isabella nodded her beautiful head coolly at Alexia, as Rafael placed a glass of champagne in her hands.

'I must congratulate you, Rafael. I didn't know you were engaged to be married.' She sipped her drink, feeling unaccountably lonely and depressed.

'There are many things about which you are ignorant,' he said blandly, with a slight smile. 'For instance, I even write some of those "sloppy love songs" you do not care for.'

Wow! she thought. I *really* got under his skin with those remarks about his career! Well, he shouldn't have been so rude and dismissive about my work. Remembering their bargain made in the car, she suppressed an urge to box his ears, and decided to drown him in honey instead.

'*Dear* Rafael,' she murmured, with a demure smile, 'I wouldn't dream of arguing with you. But I'm sure you're mistaken. How could I have used such a horrid word as "sloppy" about your wonderful, wonderful songs?'

Infuriatingly, Rafael continued to smile, albeit a bit stiffly. 'How kind of you to say so ... *dear* Alexia,' he said, in a voice every bit as sweet as hers.

'An act of pure charity—I assure you.' She fluttered her eyelashes provocatively at him. 'Especially since I've never had the ... er ... pleasure of hearing any of your songs!'

Isabella had been standing quietly, looking somewhat bewildered while this exchange took place. She was surprised to see her fiancé's face suddenly flush, a nerve rapidly beating in his temple, as the strange, lovely blonde girl smiled grimly into his dark eyes.

'Please?' said Isabella, as Rafael stalked off to replenish her drink. 'I do not understand?'

'I'm sorry,' Alexia was instantly contrite. 'It was very bad-mannered of me. I've been ... er ... teasing your fiancé, and—and I don't think he likes it very much.'

'Oh no,' agreed the girl, sighing slightly. 'Rafael is always very serious.'

'Will you be getting married soon?' asked Alexia.

Isabella shrugged her slim shoulders. 'Perhaps. I do not know.' She lapsed into a cool silence.

'Well, I hope you'll be very happy,' said Alexia, as enthusiastically as she could. Really, this girl was very beautiful, but conversationally very hard work. She was relieved when Julia came up to talk to Isabella and she could stand quietly looking around the lovely room. It was furnished with what she took to be antique Spanish furniture, the marble floor being covered with fine old rugs.

She turned to find Rafael standing silently beside her. 'Would you like another drink?' he asked, in a bland voice.

'No, thank you. I ... I've been telling Isabella that I hope you will both be very happy.'

'Like you and Luis?' he queried caustically.

Taking a deep breath, Alexia looked him straight in the eye. 'I meant it sincerely, when . . . when I wished you both happiness. Everyone has a right to be happy—even you,' she added bitterly.

She was suddenly weary of the whole conflict between her and Rafael. It had been a long day, and she felt tired and depressed. 'Luis was already a very sick man when we married,' she continued in a small voice. 'I . . . I tried to make him happy and comfortable. I . . .' she closed her lips firmly. What was the point of even bothering to explain? It was no good expecting this man, living here in the lap of luxury, to have any understanding of what it had been like, caring, nursing, and somehow trying to financially support, for four long years, a terminally ill man.

Rafael looked down at the lovely girl, whose painful memories were reflected in her green eyes. His gaze softened, as he smilingly raised his glass. 'Shall we declare a truce, Alexia?'

She smiled briefly back at him. 'Yes, please,' she said simply, blushing slightly as she caught sight of an unusual gleam in his eyes. She was grateful to be rescued from any further conversation by the announcement that dinner was ready.

Placed next to Doña Maria, who was chiefly interested in talking about her grandson, she found the truce was easily maintained, both that evening and for the next three days. Chiefly, acknowledged Alexia, thanks to the absence of Rafael.

He had shut himself away in his suite of rooms, situated in a square tower on the end of the large house. The only sign of his existence, apart from the servants carrying trays back and forth, had been the distant sight of his tall figure in a track suit, running along the beach in the early mornings.

Doña Maria had explained that he was composing some new songs for a charity concert he was due to give soon. Alexia had been surprised to learn from his mother that he not only jogged every morning, but that he exercised in a local gym for two hours every day.

'Every time he goes away on tour,' Doña Maria had said, 'he loses about six kilos—one of your English stones—in weight. It is an exhausting life, so he must keep fit . . . no?'

Julia had been staying with an old school friend along the coast and Alexia had therefore been left very much alone to read, play with Juan, and soak up the sun.

She had thought that Luis's mother would want to talk about him, but Doña Maria had been firm.

'You are looking tired and run down,' she had said firmly on the first evening after her arrival, when they had dinner alone together. 'I wish you to be fully rested before we discuss such sad things. You and I, we can talk any time. There is no need to hurry.'

The setting of the house and grounds was magnificent. Alexia had been amazed by the swimming pool, set at the end of the wide green lawn. It was surrounded by tall Greek columns, and the cliff fell away sharply to the beach below on three sides of the pool, so that to the swimmer it felt as though they were floating in the sky.

Alexia had been terrified of Juan coming to some harm, until she had seen that the cliff edge was securely, if invisibly fenced. Juan, however, preferred the small paddling pool, where he and his friends, children of the Valverdes' servants, could play happily to their hearts' content.

Her thoughts were sharply interrupted as Juan threw a bucket of cold water from the pool, against her bare back.

'Ouch! Juan ...' She jumped up laughing and began chasing the little boy around the garden, as squealing with delight, he managed to dodge her attempts to catch him.

She thought she'd lost him for a moment, and then she heard a sound around the far corner of the house. Following the grass path, she ran around a thick, dense shrub, and straight into Rafael's arms.

CHAPTER FOUR

MOMENTARILY stunned by the force of the impact, Alexia raised her startled face to see Rafael's deep blue-black eyes gleaming down at her. Once again, as had happened in his London hotel room, time seemed to be suspended between them. Gazing at each other, they stood, scarcely breathing, as she felt his arms tighten almost imperceptibly about her.

Juan's voice, calling in the distance, aroused Alexia from her trancelike state and she hurriedly stepped back as Rafael, hearing the same sound, released her from his arms.

'I'm sorry, I . . . I hope we haven't disturbed your work . . .' She was suddenly breathless and tongue-tied.

'No, not at all. This has been a charming interruption. Charming!' he repeated, stepping back to admire her bikini-clad body.

She blushed as she felt his eyes roaming over her figure. 'I—I must get dressed . . .'

'There is no need to hurry on my account,' he assured her grinningly.

'I bet there isn't,' Alexia said sourly as she turned and walked away with as much dignity as she could muster. 'Really, the man's impossible!' she muttered angrily to herself as she reached the swimming pool. Deciding she needed to cool off, both from the effect of the heat and from her encounter with Rafael, she plunged into the pool and swam two vigorous lengths before turning over to lie and float on her back, looking up at the brilliant blue sky.

It would be so wonderful here, she thought, if it weren't for Rafael. From inside the pool she could see nothing of the surrounding land—just the sea and the sky.

She really must try and not let Rafael upset her so easily. It's your own fault, she told herself sternly. You rise like a fish to the bait every single time he decides to needle you. It's obvious he doesn't like you . . . so what? You don't like him either, but there's no need to let him spoil this holiday, is there?

Having given herself a firm talking to Alexia, full of good resolutions, climbed out of the pool to find Rafael leaning nonchalantly against one of the stone columns. He gestured to a wrought iron table on which there was a tray with cups and a coffee pot.

'I felt like a break from work. Would you like to join me?'

'Why not?' she shrugged, and went over to slip on her short towelling robe. How long had he been standing there watching her she wondered, knotting her belt tightly in annoyance. Sighing inwardly, she went over to join him.

'*Que lástima!*' he said, with a disturbing gleam in his eyes. 'What a pity you have covered yourself up—you looked beautiful as you were.'

Alexia, still full of the good advice she had just given herself, stifled an urge to say something rude in reply and sat down in stony silence while he poured the coffee.

'What a surprising girl you are, Alexia. You do not like it when I pay you a compliment?'

'Why should I?' she said sarcastically. 'I'm not one of your adoring fans, fainting with ecstasy at your slightest word. Let me tell you . . .'

'No,' Rafael interrupted coldly, 'let me tell *you*. You

should learn to accept praise and not react like a startled filly, or attack like a scorpion. *Entiende?*'

Alexia sat fuming silently as he handed her a cup. He had managed to put her in the wrong yet again . . . it was all so infuriating! As for him paying her a compliment, it—it had been no such thing, and well he knew it.

'Oh, by the way,' he said blandly, ignoring her glowering silence, 'I was coming to ask you, before you threw yourself into my arms, if you would care to attend a party tonight.'

'. . . threw myself . . . into your arms?' she gasped incredulously. 'Really, how conceited can a man get? I merely bumped into you by accident . . .'

'Ah yes, "bumped" must be the right word. Please forgive me, I have not the English too good.' A mocking grin ruined the effect of his apologetic words.

'Hah!' she snorted. 'You speak "the English" perfectly, so don't bother to try that one on me!'

'How kind of you to say so. There, you see,' he laughed, 'I at least know how to accept a compliment from you.'

'It wasn't a . . . Oh! You're quite impossible!' Despite herself, Alexia grinned reluctantly back at Rafael.

'That's better,' he said approvingly. 'Now, would you like to come to a party given by a friend of mine? I would be honoured if you would accompany me.'

She regarded him warily. 'That sounds a bit more flowery than your usual style of ruthless command. What's the catch?'

'My dear Alexia, you wound me—you really do.' He shook his head mournfully. 'How can you say such a thing?'

'Very easily, Rafael, so you can take that grin off your

face.' She laughed. 'Come on . . . confess! There has to be a reason why you would want me to go with you.'

'Does there?' he said quietly. 'Could it not be that I just wished to enjoy your company?'

His suddenly serious tone of voice, together with the gleam in the dark eyes regarding her so intently, brought a slight blush to her cheeks and a disturbing flutter in her stomach.

'Will your fiancée . . . er . . . Isabella, will she be there?'

'Of course,' he said, leaning back lazily in his chair, the glint in his hooded eyes more pronounced than ever. 'Now, I wonder why you asked that question?'

I wonder why I did too, Alexia thought nervously. Why should I care if Isabella's there or not? 'Oh, you know how it is, Rafael,' she said airily.

He grinned sardonically. 'No, I do not know how it is, Alexia. Please tell me.'

Her hands itched to slap his handsome face. 'Well, the truth is,' she extemporised swiftly, 'it's a hard life, being a—a scarlet woman, I mean.' She paused for effect. 'However, if Isabella is there, I needn't worry. I can rest assured that your reputation will be quite safe. You see, I wouldn't like to embarrass you or your friends in any way,' she added in a soft voice which dripped with insincerity.

'Well done, Alexia!' He laughed and stood up. 'I note that you seem to have accepted the invitation. Be ready at eight p.m.'

She glared after his retreating figure. I bet he's good at playing chess, she mused with rueful annoyance. She might have thought she had extracted herself from an awkward corner, but he had manoeuvred her into going to the party, which was what he had intended to do from the beginning. Why?

It was a question that nagged at her off and on during the rest of the day. She and Juan had both had a siesta after their large lunch with Doña Maria, and had then gone down the path to the private beach. Juan's current craze for building sand castles had kept her gainfully employed, carting sea water and sand, until she took him, protesting, back to the house for supper and bed.

Later, standing in front of her mirror, she studied her reflection with dissatisfaction. Her dress, of soft white silk shot through with silver, shimmered as she turned. The full skirt fell from her small waist in rustling folds, while the tight cross-over bodice, fastened at the side, was cut low to display the swell of her breasts. Was it too low? she wondered anxiously, and then shrugged as she looked at her watch. It was too late to change in any case.

Dressed and ready, she hesitated. Why should she be so nervous about going to the party with Rafael? And why, for heaven's sake, should she feel so—so peculiar when she was near him? She took a deep breath to steady herself, and checking that Juan was asleep, she left her room.

'Good,' said Rafael coming into the hall as she paused at the bottom of the stairs. He gave her a swift glance from beneath his heavy eyelids. 'You are looking very beautiful tonight, Alexia,' he told her, putting an arm around her waist. 'Come along—your carriage awaits!'

She had been unable to control a nervous start at his touch, but if he noticed it, he gave no sign.

'Where's the party being held?' she asked, as he issued her into a low white sports car.

'At the Puerto Banus. Jerry Milson, the film producer, has taken over the Casino for the evening, so you can also gamble if you wish.' Rafael started the car with a roar.

'I never gamble, and neither should you,' she said absentmindedly, thankfully relieved to find that he didn't drive too fast.

He raised an eyebrow at her, quizzically. 'Why ever not?'

'Because, mathematically speaking, you're a sitting duck.' She glanced sideways at Rafael, who was wearing cream trousers and a matching cream silk shirt, with a large brown leather belt and gold buckle emphasising his slim waist. He really does look sensationally attractive, she thought idly, and then started as he said something.

'I'm sorry, I didn't hear what you said.'

'I was asking you which games of chance give the best odds.'

'None of them,' she replied promptly. 'You can win at blackjack, but it will take you a long time and you must stick to hard and fast rules. Roulette is a mug's game. Every time the ball spins it spins freshly— exactly the same as the one-armed bandits. It's really very sad to see grown men and women feeding those machines, in the pious hope that if they put in enough money the jackpot is bound to come up. You see . . . the roulette ball and the jackpot tumblers have no memory. None at all. Every time you spin the ball or pull the handle, it's as if you'd never done it before.'

She looked up to see that they had arrived. Rafael had parked the car, and was sitting looking at her with amusement.

'I'm sorry,' she blushed, 'I—I've been giving you a lecture, haven't I?'

'It was very interesting,' he answered with a warm smile. 'Tell me more.'

'Oh no,' she laughed, 'that's enough for one night. If you are interested in gambling, you should study the laws of probability.'

'Ah yes,' he said, getting out of the car and coming round to open her door. 'The laws of probability . . . very interesting.'

'I didn't know you were interested in mathematics,' she said as he took her hand to help her to rise from the low seat.

'I am discovering that it is a fascinating subject,' he said in a dry voice, keeping a firm hold of her hand as they walked towards the brilliantly-lit entrance of the Casino. 'Especially where you are concerned. I keep adding two and two and getting five for an answer!'

Alexia didn't have a chance to reply as he issued her into the building. Immediately a tall, thick-set man with an attractively craggy face appeared.

'My God, Rafael, where do you find them? Just where, for instance, did you get this simply fan-tas-tic-looking girl?' he drawled in an American accent.

'This is Jerry Milson, a film producer and our host tonight,' Rafael said to Alexia. 'Jerry, this is my sister-in-law.'

'Couldn't your husband make it tonight, honey? Never mind, I'll look after you.'

'I'm . . . I'm a widow,' said Alexia, somewhat bewildered.

'Oh God, don't I just love widows . . . they're so understanding! Get lost, Rafael! I'll get this lovely lady a drink and look after her . . . don't you worry.'

'Just behave yourself, that's all,' Rafael warned him laughingly, as he went off to greet some of his friends.

Jerry Milson took Alexia by the hand and forced a way through the throng. She found herself, minutes later, sitting on a comfortable sofa with Jerry and drinking champagne. Jerry was a mine of information about his guests and he had some interesting things to say about the films he had made. What he most wanted to talk about, however, was his unhappy marriage; his wife having left him for a boy of twenty-one.

'Fancy that,' he said, shaking his head in bewilderment. 'She's shacked up in this grim little apartment in Greenwich Village, back in New York—and you know what—she's happy. Really happy! It doesn't make sense, especially when I think how she used to scream if she didn't get a new mink coat every year.'

Alexia liked and felt sorry for the bewildered man. It was totally outside her experience of life that someone should scream for a new fur coat—but then this party was way outside anything she had ever experienced before. I wish Melanie was here, she thought suddenly. How she'd love it! Far more than I am, she sighed inwardly, feeling lonely in a sea of people she didn't know.

'You're a very nice girl, you know,' Jerry told her. 'Really very sympathetic. I've got to go and look after my guests. How about letting me buy you dinner tomorrow night, when I promise I won't bore you to death with my marital problems.'

'I'd like that,' she agreed smilingly, allowing him to lead her off to the buffet supper table where he introduced her to some other guests, among them Ty Glint, an ageing film star.

Alexia, looking around the crowded room, saw Isabella talking to another woman in the corner. Rafael didn't appear to be anywhere in sight and although Isabella wasn't looking very happy, neither did she look unhappy—just bored. The same expression she had had on her face the night of Alexia's arrival. Why should she look so fed up?

wondered Alexia. She's beautiful, she has a handsome fiancé, and will soon be married. How odd!

She turned as Ty Glint asked her if she had seen any of his films. She had to reluctantly tell him she hadn't, tactfully not mentioning that most of them had been made long before she was born.

'Come and dance,' he said, leading her out to a dimly lit patio where a small band was playing.

The setting was perfect, she thought, as they danced alone under the stars to the lilting soft music. Unfortunately, it occurred to him to try and reconstruct some of his old romantic scenes, with Alexia in a starring role. She found herself clasped tightly in a passionate embrace, having to struggle violently to avoid his equally passionate kisses. No sooner did she remove his hands from one part of her anatomy than they found another.

'Please, Mr Glint—stop it!' she pleaded tearfully, almost sagging with relief as she heard a familiar voice.

'Cut! That's the end of that scene, Ty.' She found herself released, as Rafael led the elderly man gently but firmly away.

Alexia was still trembling as Rafael returned alone, looking grim. 'If you start on at me again about being a loose woman, I'll scream the place down, Rafael! It wasn't my fault, really it wasn't. He was *awful!*' She shuddered. 'I think I'd like to go. I'll get a taxi . . .'

'*Por qué?* Surely we are about to dance?' he smiled, gently taking her into his arms. The close contact with his body caused her heart to beat rapidly, as she nervously held herself stiffly away from him, her stomach knotting with tension. As they moved slowly over the floor, she noticed that other couples had joined them out on the patio. There didn't seem to be much dancing, however, as each pair stood entwined with each other swaying to the music.

'Relax, Alexia,' Rafael murmured, his eyes glinting in the dim light as he firmly placed her arms about his neck. 'You are quite safe!'

She didn't feel at all safe as he drew her closer to his hard figure, placing his arms lightly but firmly about her soft body. She could feel the warmth of his skin through the soft silk shirt, her heart pounding fiercely as he placed his cool cheek next to hers.

'You see, it is not so very terrible, Alexia,' he whispered, his warm lips softly kissing her ear. She seemed to be losing any ability to think coherently, as, trapped within his arms, she felt herself surrendering to the rising tide of trembling excitement which was beginning to pulse through her veins.

As he gently ran his lips across her cheek, she gasped as his mouth touched a corner of hers. Softly and delicately he explored the outline of her lips with a tenderly sensual, delicate touch that made her senses reel. She felt as if she was drowning as his warm, firm mouth became more insistent, moving over her lips and forcing them apart, and she was convulsed by a raging storm of desire, trembling violently in the grip of an emotion she had never before experienced.

With a convulsive shudder, his body shaking in response to the trembling, quivering figure in his arms, Rafael moved his hands to place them either side of her head. Slowly and reluctantly he withdrew his mouth, looking down at her eyes glowing with languorous desire, the soft temptation of her lips.

'*Por Dios*, Alexia!' he groaned softly as she clung to him, helplessly caught and enmeshed by a force she couldn't control. His dark head descended to tenderly possess her lips again, his arms moving to tighten convulsively about her slim figure.

It was some time before they realised that the music had ended. Alexia was so shaken that she would have fallen without the support of his arm about her waist, as he led her silently towards an empty table. Collapsing on to a chair, she trembled nervously as Rafael lifted two glasses from the tray of a passing waiter. She glanced through eyelashes that still quivered from the assault on her senses, at his pale stern face and the unfathomable expression in the dark, hooded eyes regarding her so intently. She blushed, a deep crimson tide spreading across her face as she recollected, with horrified shame, the behaviour of her treacherous body. Totally at a loss for words, completely incapable of saying anything, she buried her nose in the champagne to hide her confusion.

Rafael, looking at the flushed girl whose hands trembled so much that she could hardly hold her glass, nervously cleared his throat. He was clearly about to speak when a group of people spilled through on to the patio from the room beyond.

'Come on, Rafael, time for you to sing,' they cried. He protested, but as they refused to take 'no' for an answer, he cast a rueful look at Alexia and allowed himself to be led away to a piano.

Standing out on the patio, Alexia watched as the guests crowded into the main room to listen. Unable to stop herself, she drifted over to the open door and leant against a stone pillar looking over the heads of the seated guests. Rafael sat facing her idly playing some chords, waiting until everyone had settled themselves comfortably around him.

Across the room she saw Isabella chatting to a young man. Once again, she thought, the girl looked exquisite, yet listless. Maybe that's just her expression, thought Alexia with a pang of guilt, remembering just how she had been dancing with the girl's fiancé. You've behaved shamefully, she told herself in disgust as Rafael began to sing.

It was his latest chart-topper, 'Give Me Your Love' and the aching sweetness of his voice made her legs tremble. He's affecting every other woman in the room in exactly the same way, she told herself desperately; but it did nothing to assuage the throbbing ache of unsatisfied desire that racked her body.

Confused, she wandered around the patio and then walked slowly back to the deserted bar, where a waiter was serving a solitary figure.

'*Hola!*' The man turned to look at the pale, beautiful girl. 'Will you join me?'

She nodded silently, and climbed up on a stool beside the stranger.

'This is unusual—a lovely woman who isn't listening to Rafael. Maybe I should be worried?'

Alexia looked at the plump, middle-aged Spaniard, who was smiling so kindly at her. She really didn't feel like talking to anyone ... anyone at all. Why couldn't he just go away and leave her alone? She sighed as he handed her a glass of wine.

'Why should you worry, *señor*?' she asked.

'Well, you see, my dear young lady, I am producing Rafael's charity concert next week,' he said with a smile. 'It would be sad if the women didn't listen to him any more. Very sad, financially!'

She gave him a rueful, shaky smile. 'I don't think you have much to fear. The room next door is littered with women who seem to have a glazed look in their eyes!'

'*Esta muy bien.* Good ... my job sounds safer.' He paused to listen with his head on one side, to the different tune Rafael was now playing in the outer room. 'This is a traditional melody of our country. He has given it some new words. It is nice.'

'Do you produce all his concerts, *señor?*' Alexia asked, desperately trying not to listen to the caressing voice next door.

'Only in Spain. We have come a long way, Rafael and I. Oh yes, a long way.' He ordered a brandy for himself while she smilingly refused another glass of wine.

'Have you known him a long time?'

'*Si*, since his days at Madrid University. He studied the law. They said he would be a famous lawyer, like his father. Life is strange, is it not?'

'I don't quite understand . . .' she frowned.

'Aha! It is simple . . . no? Rafael's family is very old . . . that is good. But his father died when he was at university, and the family have no money . . . that is bad. So the boy, he begins to sing at night clubs to help the family. It is a slow beginning, of course, you understand. But then . . . poof! Everyone goes mad for Rafael. I sell my night club, and we are in business.' He beamed at Alexia. 'Now he makes so much money he can support the family—and the cousins and the aunts and the grandparents—all the relatives. Oh yes, Rafael has been a good boy to his family. He is a good man.'

'But what about his law career? It must have been difficult . . . it must have been hard for him to have to give it up, surely?'

He shrugged. '*Es posible*. He never speaks about it. It is not, how do you say, "practical" to think about what cannot be.' He laughed. 'Of course, he looks at his contracts very, very carefully!'

Alexia smiled, but she felt a deep pang of sympathetic understanding for Rafael. She too had been forced to sacrifice her desires and ambitions on the altar of family duty. She knew exactly what it felt like to suppress one's hopes and aspirations for the good of others.

For the first time since she had met him, Alexia began to see Rafael as a human being, not as the authoritarian figure whom she had disliked and with whom she was so often in conflict. Oh dear, she thought sadly, I've been as guilty of blind prejudice as he has. No wonder he had reacted so sharply to her accusation about 'poncing about on a stage'—she winced at the memory of her cruel words.

The strains of a different tune came through the open door and they both listened for a moment.

'That must be one of Rafael's new songs, I have not heard it before. He tells me he has been composing some new material for his next show. It sounds good . . . yes?'

She listened to the mournful notes and soft, echoing voice as the haunting melody caught at her heart-strings. 'It's . . . it's lovely,' she said slowly. 'I can't understand the Spanish words, of course, but it's a lovely tune.'

The producer listened for a moment, as he got down from the bar stool. 'He is singing: "Who are you . . . really? What are you . . . really?" He paused. '"You have entered my life . . . and you have bewitched me." It will do well. Yes, he has a new hit, I think.'

'Yes,' she whispered, 'I'm sure he has.'

Alexia was lost in her own confused thoughts, as the other guests started coming back to the bar and her new acquaintance bade her farewell. A moment later she found her arm grasped by Rafael.

'I have sung for my supper. We are leaving now.'

Glancing sideways at his stern, blank face, she

slipped off her stool. 'I—I must thank Jerry for his party . . .'

'There is no need,' he said, propelling her firmly in front of him. 'I have already said our thanks.'

'What about ... surely you—you should take Isabella home? I can easily take a taxi. I . . .'

'I don't want any arguments from you, Alexia. Into the car,' he said firmly, holding the door open.

The journey back to the house was conducted in silence, her nerves strung to fever pitch as they came to a halt outside the front door. Rafael glanced at the trembling girl beside him.

'We must talk, you and I.' His voice was harsh as his hands tightened on the driving wheel.

'No, I . . .' She swiftly opened the car door and jumped out. 'Please ... I can't. I'm really very sorry ... I ... Oh, Rafael, I'm so ashamed!' Swiftly she ran through the front door and up the stairs to her room, throwing herself on to the bed in an agonising turmoil of emotional confusion.

CHAPTER FIVE

'HELLO . . . I'm back!' Julia danced into Alexia's room, where she sat in her dressing gown sipping her morning coffee, the toast on her breakfast tray lying untouched before her. 'I got back yesterday evening. Have you missed me?'

Alexia smiled wanly at the exuberant girl. 'Of course I have. Did you have a good time with your friends?'

'Yes, great. Still, it's good to be back. I wondered if you'd like to come shopping with me this morning? I see you've decided to have breakfast up here today.'

'Well, Rosa collected Juan, and I—I didn't feel quite up to going downstairs . . .' Alexia's voice trailed away.

'Very wise,' agreed Julia. 'It has not been what you might call a happy family meal this morning. Rafael has been snapping everyone's head off—even Mama's. He's in a really foul mood, I can tell you. Take my advice and stay well clear of him.'

'Oh, I shall,' agreed Alexia fervently. 'I'd love to come shopping with you, if you don't mind Juan coming too.'

'Oops, I forgot! Mamá asked if he could go with her to meet some of her friends' grandchildren. It's a lunch party for tiny tots, given by the grannies.' Julie laughed. 'Mamá is so thrilled to belong to the grandmothers' club at last—now she feels one hundred per cent respectable!'

Alexia smiled. 'Tell your mother that she's very

welcome to take Juan—I just hope he doesn't tire her out, that's all. I'll just have a shower and get dressed. I'll try not to keep you waiting long.'

'No hurry,' said Julia, going off to see her mother.

Half an hour later Alexia sat at her dressing table, looking at her face in despair. The deep shadows beneath her large green eyes were clear evidence of her sleepless night. Applying a thicker make-up than usual seemed to make little difference.

It's just sex, she told herself, for the hundredth time since she had returned last night. S-E-X. According to books and magazines, it happens to everyone, all the time. It's just that it hadn't happened to her . . . until now that was. How ridiculous, she thought, to have reached the age of twenty-three before being hit for six like this. It would be laughable, only somehow she seemed to have lost her sense of humour.

You're just another victim of Rafael's well-known charm. You're like all the other women who lust after him. Lust—that's a good biblical word, very descriptive, she thought, as she continued to mentally berate herself.

She started to brush her hair vigorously. She must start thinking clearly and logically. She always had done so, and this was no time to stop. Firstly, she must keep well away from Rafael. She seemed to have caught some sort of infectious disease that affected every woman, between the ages of eight and eighty, with whom he came into contact. He should be locked up, she thought bitterly, he wasn't safe to have around!

Secondly, thirdly and fourthly, she mustn't let him guess how she felt about him. She didn't know why this was so important—but it was. Maybe it's my pride, she mused unhappily. Whatever the reason, she was determind not to join all the other adoring women. He's conceited and arrogant enough as it is, besides which, she told herself defiantly, you don't even like the man. In fact, you hate him!

Lastly . . . she stopped brushing her hair as she felt a pang of real guilt and shame. Isabella! How would I like it if my fiancé was having a smoochy dance with another woman? I'd hate it! No wonder the poor girl always looked so fed up. She's probably spent countless, sleepless nights crying over that Casanova she's engaged to. What a swine he is!

She leaned her chin on her hands and looked at herself in the mirror. That's all very well, my girl, but *you* didn't run screaming from the dance floor, did you? You didn't get upset with Rafael like you did with Ty Glint . . . oh no!

Alexia's face flushed and she trembled, remembering the feel of Rafael's arms about her. His hard, lean body, his mouth on hers . . .

'Are you ready?' Julia came into the room.

'What? . . . oh . . . oh yes, nearly. It's just my hair . . .'

'It's lovely, Alexia. You ought to wear it long like that always.'

'Heavens, no! It's so thick . . . besides, I'm too old for that sort of hairdo. I thought I'd get it cut while I'm out here. What do you think?'

'No, you mustn't!' Julia looked appalled. 'And how can you say you're too old? You're so beautiful. How silly you are!'

Julia drove with speed and verve into Marbella, and took Alexia with her to the Fish Market.

'The housekeeper asked me to get her some *boquerones*—anchovies—for supper. I love coming here early in the morning,' she added. 'The stalls are full of the most beautiful fish, all freshly caught. There's not much left by this time in the day.'

'What's that?' asked Alexia, pointing to what looked like small white rubber tubing.

'That's *calamares*—squid.'

'Ugh!'

'No, it is delicious. I will ask Mamá to have some for dinner one night, you will love it.'

'Oh no, I won't,' laughed Alexia, 'so you can forget that idea straight away!'

'I can see that you are a coward, Alexia,' Julia grinned. 'I had a year at school in England, and I had to eat tripe. Ugh! It was disgusting. So you see, I will have no pity for you when you have to swallow some squid!'

Laughing and joking, Julia led the way from the Fish Market into the Orange Square. 'Would you like some coffee?' she asked, weaving her way through the people seated at the white tables and chairs among the orange trees, narrowly avoiding a hovering waiter who was carrying a large tray of drinks.

'I'd love some,' Alexia sighed with pleasure as she sat down at an empty table. 'This is so pretty, Julia,' she gestured around her at the white buildings and the gaily striped awnings over the shops.

'Yes, it is nice, and I love spending the summer down here. However, you must come and stay with us in Madrid. It is such a beautiful city . . . I am sure you will like it.'

A man walking through the square caught sight of Alexia's blonde head, and quickly retraced his steps towards the two girls.

'Alexia,' he smiled. 'It seems we've met up rather sooner than I thought we would. How are you?'

'Michael! How lovely to see you. Come and join us.

This is Michael West, Julia. You must be very nice to him, because not only is he one of my oldest friends, but he's also one of my best customers!'

Julia looked up at the tall, fair-haired and handsome Englishman. 'It will be a pleasure,' she said, her eyes sparkling.

'What have you been up to in Spain, Alexia? Are you enjoying your holiday?'

'I'm staying with Luis's family,' she explained, 'and having a marvellously lazy time.'

'Ah yes, I remember you told me in London. So,' he turned to Julia, 'you are Alexia's sister-in-law? Are you down here on holiday too?'

They were chatting and ordering more coffee when Julia suddenly waved and called to someone behind Alexia.

'It is Isabella,' she cried gaily. 'She must come over and join us. *Otro café con leche, por favor,*' she called out to a passing waiter.

Oh lord! thought Alexia, that's all I need this morning. Isabella, of all people!

Julia greeted the girl enthusiastically and introduced her to Michael West. Alexia was so preoccupied with her own feelings of guilt regarding Isabella that she sat silently for a while before turning to speak to Michael. She was surprised to find him staring at Isabella as if he had seen a vision. Well, maybe he has, she thought, looking at the Spanish girl as she chatted to Julia. Even in the clear light of day, her flawless beauty seemed to light up the square. She's perfect, thought Alexia, suddenly feeling tired and depressed, absolutely perfect. Rafael must be mad about her, and . . . and who could blame him?

'We have to go,' said Julia reluctantly. 'I arranged to go riding and spend the day with some friends, so I

must get back to change. I know,' she turned to
Michael, 'why don't you come to lunch tomorrow?'

'Fine, I'd like that.' He turned to Isabella. 'Will you
. . . er . . . will you be there too?'

'Of course you'll come—won't you, Isabella?' Julia
echoed the invitation. 'Come early, and bring your
swimming things. It will be great fun.'

Isabella blushed, and nodded with a smile.

Well! thought Alexia, as she followed Julia back to the
car. That's the first sign of life I've seen in that girl since I
arrived. She looked over her shoulder at Michael and
Isabella as they sat still talking at the table. He certainly
seemed smitten, she thought as she waved goodbye.

The rest of the day passed quietly. Julia had
dropped her off at the house before going to join her
friends. Juan and Doña Maria were also out, as was
Rafael. The housekeeper said it was no trouble to
provide her with a picnic and she decided to spend the
day on the beach.

She was walking back across the lawn to the house
in the late afternoon, feeling pleasantly relaxed, when
Rosa appeared at a french window.

'*El telefono, señora,*' she called.

'For me?' Alexia was surprised.

'*Si, si, señora.*'

It was Jerry Milson. 'Hi, kid, did you remember our
date tonight?'

'Oh yes . . . of course,' she said brightly, having
completely forgotten last night's invitation.

'Great. I'll pick you up at eight o'clock, then. 'Bye.'

She was reading a story to Juan, who seemed to
have had a wonderful time with his grandmother,
when she heard a car draw up outside the house.

She kissed the boy goodnight. 'I've got to go now,
darling. Sleep well.'

The ring of the door bell brought Rafael from the study as she reached the bottom of the stairs.

'Are you going out?' he asked in a hard voice, gazing intently at Alexia who was looking very beautiful in a slim black dress which showed off her deepening tan.

'Yes, yes, I am,' she said nervously as he stood staring at her.

'Who with?' he demanded harshly.

'Really!' she exclaimed, her hackles rising at his tone. 'With Jerry Milson, if you must know. Anyway, it's none of your damn business,' she added, as the bell rang again.

'Hah!' Rafael snorted angrily, striding back into the study and slamming the door loudly behind him.

'It's been a lovely evening,' said Alexia, as Jerry drove her home in his large American car. 'But it's awfully late. You shouldn't have persuaded me to that last game of backgammon.'

'I know I shouldn't . . . you beat me hollow!'

Alexia laughed at his mournful tone. It had been an amusing evening. First a meal of delicious Spanish food and then Jerry had taken her to a bar, where they had settled down to talk mainly about his wife. Some people sitting at the next table had been playing backgammon, and when she told Jerry she had never learnt the game, he had called for a board and insisted on teaching her.

'Here we are,' he said, as they arrived back at the Valverde house. 'It's been really fun. Let's do it again some time.'

'I'd like that,' she said as he gave her a friendly peck on the cheek before driving away.

Goodness, she thought, looking at her watch in the light of the porch, it's two o'clock! Opening the front door, which squeaked noisily, she began to feel her way around the dark hall, to the staircase.

She gave a startled cry as the study door opened and a hand grabbed her arm, pulling her none too gently into the dimly lit room.

'My God! What . . .'

'Do you realise what the time is?' Rafael demanded in a furious voice.

'Of course I do. How dare you scare me like that!' She was trembling with fright. 'I—I might have had a heart attack!' she gasped, sinking down on to a velvet-covered sofa.

He looked searchingly at her ashen face, then turned to walk over to a drinks tray in the corner of the room. 'Here, you'd better have a brandy,' he said, handing her a glass which she held tightly in her shaking hands. 'Now,' he said sternly, 'where have you been and what have you been doing?'

'It—it's got nothing to do with you how I spend my time. What's this supposed to be . . . the Spanish Inquisition?' Her hands were still trembling, but as much from his close proximity as he stood glaring down at her, as from the fright she had just sustained.

'It is disgraceful that you should be out so late . . . and with such a man.'

'Jerry? What's wrong with him. He's very nice. He's just unhappy about his wife, that's all.'

'And you consoled him, eh? In your usual manner, I suppose?'

'What!' Alexia gasped incredulously. 'What in the hell are you talking about? Are you suggesting that . . . that I . . .' She almost choked with rage, as she stared up at his grimly set and angry face. 'You can't seriously suggest that I would . . . why, I hardly know the man . . . I . . .' She jumped to her feet to face him, trembling with fury. 'You're unbelievable . . . you really are! You seem to have this completely mad idea that I'm some sort of ... some sort of nymphomaniac!' She laughed wildly, as she tossed back the full glass of brandy, nearly choking as the fiery liquid burnt her throat.

'Actually,' she said bitterly, suddenly feeling light-headed, 'you're absolutely right. What really happened was that I went down to the Port and ran up and down the quay, calling out: "Come and get me, boys—it's free tonight!" Oh yes I'm known as Good Time Alexia—didn't you know?'

Rafael's lips began to twitch as he took the empty glass from her hand. 'I think giving you that brandy was a mistake,' he murmured wryly.

'You know something? I really hate and despise you! I had a nice quiet evening out with a nice man, and now you ... with your—your filthy mind ... you've spoilt everything!'

'Oh, Alexia,' he put a hand on her shoulder, 'I ...'

'Don't you dare touch me, you ... you damn dago!' she cried hysterically, swinging her arm up to slap his face as hard as she could.

She was shocked at her violent action and horrified to see, as Rafael stood motionless, the imprint of her hand beginning to glow on his pale face.

They stood glaring at each other for a moment, before he gave her a hard push which sent her tumbling back on to the sofa, while he calmly put her glass on a table before coming to sit down beside her.

Her startled green eyes widened in fright as he raised his hand, flinching as she waited for the retaliatory blow. Instead of which, he calmly removed the combs which held her hair in place and shook the thick curly tresses free about her shoulders.

'Leave my hair alone!' she snapped furiously. 'What do you think you're doing? Oh no!—*No!*'

Taking no notice of her protests, Rafael slipped
one arm about her waist and leaning over her,
buried his other hand in her hair, forcing her head
back. There was nothing she could do to avoid the
slow, deliberate descent of his head, neither could
she evade his mouth, which possessed hers in a
hard, brutal kiss.

She tried to fight him, her hands beating wildly
against his hard body, as he pinned her firmly down
against the cushions of the sofa. Her struggles became
weaker and she realised that she was completely at his
mercy, as he ruthlessly savaged the full softness of her
mouth.

Unable to move, she felt as though she was slipping
into a dark void of unconsciousness, when his mouth
gradually eased its pressure and she began to shiver
involuntarily as his lips began a sensual exploration of
her mouth.

She was powerless to resist the answering flame
which the soft seduction of his lips ignited within her,
and which grew to fill her whole trembling body.
Relaxing his firm hold, he ran his mouth gently over
her face, whispering softly in Spanish as he kissed her
closed eyelids, before his mouth trailed down her
cheek to possess her lips again.

The tantalising sweetness of his kiss brought an
instinctive response she was unable to control. Her
fingers convulsively buried themselves in his hair, and
she moaned softly as she felt his hands moving over
her body.

His experienced fingers swiftly undid the buttons of
her dress, and she gave a startled gasp as he found and
began to caress her swollen breast. Slowly withdrawing
his mouth, he looked down into her green eyes, whose
gold flecks flickered in the dim light. Her eyelids

fluttered nervously as she gazed sightlessly back at him, lost in a deep mist of passionate desire.

'*Dios!* Sweet mother of God—how I want you!' he groaned, burying his mouth in the hollow of her throat, before running his lips over her golden skin to the rising swell of her creamy breast.

The sound of his voice broke through her unconscious, bemused state. As she felt his lips on her breast and became aware of an increasing urgency in his body, she came back with a bump to harsh reality. Reality and shame.

'Oh God! No, Rafael . . . No!' she cried huskily, as in a blind panic she began to struggle. Fear lent her strength and caught off guard, he let her go.

Alexia stumbled to her feet, staggering to a desk by a window where with her back to him, she feverishly tried to do up her dress. It took some moments for her trembling fingers to manage the buttons, before she slumped down in a chair to bury her face in her hands.

Her face burned with shame as waves of humiliation assailed her. It was hopeless to try and explain to him that never before had anyone kissed her, or touched her body like that . . . Rafael seemed convinced that she was a promiscuous woman, and had treated her as such. Her body still throbbed with desire, and suddenly it all became too much for her to cope with as great racking sobs shook her frame.

She felt her hands being grasped and Rafael gently raised her to her feet, holding her lightly in his arms while she sobbed against his shoulder.

'I'm sorry . . . I . . .' she hiccuped, her voice still husky with the passion he had aroused. Haltingly, she raised her large eyes swimming with tears to his. 'I'm . . . I'm so ashamed of myself . . . and you. I feel so . . . so humiliated! I . . .' she broke off, trying to collect herself. 'I know it's a waste of time to tell you, yet again, that I'm not a loose woman. But surely a man of your ... your sexual experience ... surely you must know that I'm not!' she cried bitterly.

'Oh, Alexia,' he whispered, gently brushing the damp curly tendrils from her forehead. '*Lo siento, lo siento mucho!* I'm truly sorry. Of course I ... yes, of course—of course I know. I ...' He buried his face in the fragrant cloud of her hair as his arms tightened about her.

'Dear God—no!' she cried, appalled to find, as he held her closely to him, that her body was beginning to betray her once again. She backed nervously away from him, her tortured eyes gazing at his face, pale beneath its dark tan. 'All you've proved tonight, Rafael, is that I'm just a weak, stupid woman who's easily capable of being seduced. That's—that's my problem, and I'll have to live with the humiliating thought. But—but surely,' she said, anger coming to her aid, 'surely you have enough women crazy over you? There are all those fans, and—and you're engaged to be married to the most beautiful girl I've ever seen! Surely that's enough, even for you, without having to add my scalp to your belt?'

'*Ah no, querida,*' he protested anxiously.

'You've accused me of the most vile behaviour, but—but what about yours? My God, I really pity Isabella! If this is how you behave now, heaven help the poor girl when you're married,' she said scathingly.

'Alexia!' he groaned. 'It's—it's not like that ... you must understand!'

'I—I don't want to understand. I'm going to my room now,' she said angrily, blinking away the tears which threatened to fall again. 'Not only are you a swine of the first order, but if I never saw you again, it would be too soon—believe me!' she cried, running blindly to the door.

As she lay in her bath the next morning, for the first time in her life, Alexia's tired mind refused to function normally. The physical and mental assault on her emotions of the last evening had led to her lying awake most of the night in mental torture. At one moment she would be consigning Rafael to the eternal flames of damnation, while the next she would find herself recalling the touch of his firm mouth and the feel of his hands on her body.

Exhausted, she had dozed off as dawn approached, only to be woken by Julia, who laughingly chided her for having overslept. It was eleven o'clock, and their guests would be arriving soon. Even worse, Alexia thought, she was neglecting Juan, although Julia had assured her he was happy in the paddling pool with his friends.

'If you don't mind me saying so, Alexia, you look terrible! Why not have a long bath, and I'll pop up later to see how you feel.'

'I—I don't mind. You're quite right, I must look ghastly. I—I didn't sleep last night—it must be the heat. Please don't worry I'll have a bath and be down soon.'

Lying in the warm, scented water, Alexia found herself still sunk in deep depression. She'd have to stagger through the lunch party somehow. With any luck Rafael wouldn't be present, and at least it would be nice to see Michael again. The thought of seeing her old friend made her feel slightly more cheerful, as she stepped out of the bath.

Hearing a knock on the door of her bedroom, she

grabbed a small towel and holding it sketchily in front of her, opened the bathroom door.

'Come in, Julia,' she called, walking into her room. 'I'm just going to get dressed, it won't take me long to . . .' She gasped, frozen with horror as she saw Rafael close the door behind him. 'What—what are you doing here?' she demanded angrily.

'I came to apologise for last night,' he said stiffly. 'I behaved very badly towards you and . . .' his voice trailed away as his eyes devoured her naked body, inadequately covered by the small towel.

Blushing a deep red under his gaze, she tried, with little succes, to cover her anatomy.

'We—we both know that you're no gentleman,' she snapped contemptuously, 'but will you please turn around and—and allow me to put on my dressing gown?'

He flinched visibly at her words, but silently did as she asked. Alexia looked doubtfully at the back of his tall figure for a moment, as he studiously gazed at a picture on the wall in front of him. Then she quickly grabbed her thin silk gown which lay on a nearby chair, wrapping it tightly around her and swiftly knotting the belt.

'You can stop looking at that picture now,' she said coldly.

He turned slowly and leant against the wall with his arms folded, as they gazed silently at each other.

Oh lord! she thought, feeling sick with nerves, as she looked at his tall, handsome figure. Her heart began to thud and she closed her eyes for a moment, the burning knot of tension in her stomach spreading through every fibre of her being.

Rafael cleared his throat, unable to say anything as he looked at the beautiful girl, dressed only in the silk wrap which clung so tightly to her damp figure. She was completely unaware that her full breasts, their swollen rosy tips thrusting against the thin, diaphanous material, presented a far more provocative sight than the small towel had done.

'H-hum,' he cleared his throat again. 'Alexia,' he said huskily, 'I must ask you to forgive me for—for what happened last night.' He walked over to stand looking out of the window. 'I—I behaved very badly. You are a guest in my home, and I—I am very sorry.' He turned to face the trembling girl. 'It was just a—a moment of madness, believe me. It meant nothing.'

'If it meant nothing to you, I'd be fascinated to know how you behave when you do feel something!' she flashed back angrily before she could stop herself. Mortified, she bit her lip at having so clearly exposed her raw emotion. Of course it meant nothing to him . . . the beast! Women must fall into his hands like ripe apples, she told herself bitterly. She strove manfully for a calmness she didn't feel.

'All right, Rafael,' she said at last, 'I—I will accept your apology. And—and I won't mention anything to Isabella,' she added with malicious spite. 'So you needn't worry about that—you're quite safe!'

'It never occurred to me . . .' he answered angrily.

'Well, it had better occur to you!' she snapped at him with contempt. 'Because the next time you feel like a—a little "moment of madness", the girl may very well shout "Rape" loudly and—and run to Isabella or the newspapers. With your sexual appetite, it looks like a short marriage and an even shorter career!'

'*My sexual appetite?*' Rafael thundered angrily, his face a mask of fury. 'You know nothing about me!'

'Oh yes, I do!' she shouted back, completely losing

control. No one's safe around you . . . no one! You're a—a damned menace!'

'I'm a what . . .?' he snarled, shaking with rage. 'Who are you, you stupid girl—who are you to say . . .'

'Me? I'm the stupid sister-in-law, that's who! And—and what's more, I'm—I'm extremely well qualified to talk about your sexual appetite. Your brother had hardly been buried, before you'd grabbed and assaulted me. And—and laughed about it! My God, you should be locked up!' She burst into wild hysterical laughter.

'Stop it! *Bastante!* Stop it at once!' he shouted, striding forward and slapping her face.

Reeling back from the blow, she stared at him shocked and dazed, her eyes large green pools of stricken misery.

'*Ah, perdone . . . perdone, mi Alexia!*' he groaned. Drawing her thinly clad figure slowly into his arms, he gently kissed each sad eyelid before sliding his mouth down her cheek to take possession of her lips, teasing them with such a gentle pressure, that unconsciously she strained towards him, her arms creeping slowly up to wind themselves about his neck.

'You are driving me insane,' he breathed, his mouth brushing and tantalising her trembling lips, as his hands slipped over the silk gown, tenderly caressing her soft body.

'Rafael . . .' she gasped, swept by a great surge of desire, her senses drugged and seduced into quivering acquiescence by the pounding of his heart which was beating as rapidly as her own, the warm, musky scent of his body.

A deep shudder shook his frame, as with a muffled groan he responded to the innocently erotic provocation of the trembling figure in his arms. His kiss deepened, his lips becoming ever more demanding and possessive.

Deeply locked in their mutual passion as they were, it was some moments before they realised that they were not alone. Alexia looked up startled, her gasp of dismay alerting Rafael. He turned to see Rosa, with a tray in her hand, beaming at them.

Alexia, paralysed by the swift turn of events, stood shaking with apprehension while Rosa and Rafael spoke rapidly to each other in Spanish. Finally Rosa laughingly shook her head, and gestured that he must go.

'*Marchese, marchese, Rafael!*' she said. With a rueful shrug he kissed Alexia briefly on the forehead and left the room.

Quite bewildered, Alexia turned her startled eyes to Rosa, who smiled at her and put the cup of coffee down on the table.

'Oh, Rosa . . . I . . .' she swallowed nervously. What could she say? And why wasn't the old nanny angry to have found them . . . well, the way she had?

'*Ea!*' Rosa laughed. 'Much noise, much fight and much passion! *Bueno!*'

Bueno? Surely '*bueno*' meant good? 'But, Rosa, it is not *bueno*. It is bad, very bad,' she said unhappily.

'Is no bad,' the old nanny said firmly. 'I tell him he need a woman with fire. Much trouble for him, but also much passion . . . no?' She left the room cackling with laughter.

CHAPTER SIX

ALEXIA let the grains of golden sand trickle through her fingers, as she idly watched a small crab scuttle for safety under a rock. Apart from Juan, busily engaged by the water's edge in digging out a moat for his sandcastle, the beach and the coastline of the bay was completely deserted.

The sand shimmered in the haze of the early afternoon sun, Alexia sighing as she contemplated the beautiful scene. The last three days of peace and quiet had done much to restore her battered spirits. She might have many problems—God knows she had—but it was impossible to remain in a permanent state of gloom, surrounded as she was by golden sands and azure blue sky.

Rafael had been away since the lunch party at the recording studios in Madrid, according to Julia. Since his departure, Alexia's days had been a mixture of wandering around Marbella, or the neighbouring small town of San Pedro de Alcantara, with Julia and Juan in the mornings, and lazy afternoons spent on the beach.

If only the rest of the holiday could be like this! Peaceful, quiet . . . and safe. The thought of Rafael's return tomorrow brought up to the surface all the feelings she had been repressing these last few days. Of course she didn't want him back, with the renewal of the tension and the emotional turmoil he always seemed to engender within her . . . of course she didn't . . . Alexia sighed with perplexity. So why then did the thought of his arrival make her feel sick with excitement? It was all so complicated and she really didn't understand it at all . . .

In spite of Alexia's conviction that the lunch party could only be a disaster, the presence of Michael, together with that of Rafael's producer and his publicity manager, ensured that it was not . . . at least not—not until the end.

Playing the part of an urbane host to perfection, Rafael projected such an aura of warm, friendly charm as he moved among his family and guests, that if she hadn't known better, Alexia could have sworn the scene upstairs earlier that morning had been a complete figment of her imagination.

She had been standing talking quietly to Michael before lunch, when Rafael had approached with his producer.

'Ah, Alexia . . . good morning. Julia tells me that you didn't sleep well. It must be the heat. I trust you are feeling better now?' he asked blandly.

She murmured something inaudible, burying her nose in her glass of Sangria. Really! The effrontery of the man! How he was able to pretend that nothing had happened . . . Don't be stupid, she told herself fiercely, nothing had happened . . . nothing as far as he's concerned, that is.

'I'd like you to meet Alfonso. He produces some of my shows, and . . .'

'*Buenos dias*, dear lady,' said the man she had met at Jerry's party. 'We meet again.'

'You know my sister-in-law?' Rafael looked surprised.

'Oh yes. She is a remarkable person, you know. She was the only woman who wasn't listening to you at the Casino. No, she preferred to talk to me in the bar. It made my evening . . . *absolutamente*!'

Rafael's hooded eyes flashed briefly. 'Well, it would seem, Alfonso, that she is a lady of taste and judgment, would it not?' he drawled smoothly, before turning to see to his other guests.

Oh heavens! I don't think I'm going to be able to hack my way through this lunch, Alexia groaned inwardly. Now he thinks I don't like his singing . . . on top of all the other things I said . . .

Seeing that Alfonso was busily talking to Michael, she turned to stare blindly at a picture on the wall, while she fought to control the sudden surge of misery that threatened to engulf her.

'It's a charming oil painting, but I don't think it deserves quite the attention you are giving it!' Rafael's voice spoke softly behind her. 'Here, let me fill your glass.'

She turned slowly, watching while he poured the glowing red liquid into her glass from a jug topped with slices of orange and lemon.

'It wasn't that I didn't like your singing . . . It—it was just that I was upset that night. I mean . . .' she floundered helplessly. Why, in heaven's name was she bothering to try and explain? She blushed unhappily.

'*No importa*,' he said dismissively. 'I do remember that evening, you know. I remember it very well,' he added quietly, running a slim, tanned finger down one side of her face and tilting her chin up towards him. 'What is the immortal English phrase: "Up, Guards, and at 'em"? So cheer up . . . and chin up, Alexia!'

He turned to address the guests. 'Come on, everybody, I think lunch is ready,' he called, issuing them into the dining room.

The lunch passed smoothly, course following course. Alexia talked determinedly and brightly to Alfonso, studiously ignoring Rafael at the end of the table.

Julia was full of the masked ball to be held at a large night club nearby. 'Everyone has to wear masks. It's going to be such fun, Rafael, please can we go?'

'Oh, Julia, do we have to?' he groaned with a wry smile. 'Surely you would prefer to stay quietly at home?'

'You must be joking! Oh, come on, do say you'll take us. It will do you good to go out for an evening, for once.'

'My dear girl, I spend a good part of my life "out for the evening", as you put it.'

'That's work,' she said firmly. 'You should also play . . . shouldn't he, Isabella?'

The Spanish girl, who had been talking to Michael, looked at Julia and shrugged. 'Rafael will please himself, will he not?'

'Well, I'm going to please myself,' said Julia defiantly. 'I shall just go on my own, that's all.'

'No!' Rafael spoke firmly and forceably. 'I will not allow it. It is entirely unsuitable that a girl of your age should do so.' He sighed dramatically. 'It seems that for peace and quiet, I shall have to give in. Very well, we will make up a party for the evening. I must say, the thought of having to wear a mask appals me. Michael you had better come to lend me your support. Alfonso?'

'Oh no!' Rafael's producer laughed. 'Trying to disguise myself? With my face and figure? Absolutely not. I'm much too old for that sort of thing.' He went off into peals of laughter.

'Tough luck, *viejo amigo*! You've been drafted,' said Rafael with a grim smile.

Alexia had been following this exchange with some bewilderment, astonished to find that Rafael did not seem to be much of a partygoer. She had supposed he spent much of his life at wild parties, surrounded by beautiful women. Maybe he did, and it was just that his young sister did not know of his activities. Isabella was acting oddly, too. Her lacklustre approach to her fiancé was difficult to comprehend, especially as she was laughing and smiling at Michael as he regaled her with a long, involved story about a mishap on his flight to Spain.

Throughout the meal Alexia had also been puzzled by the smiles and grins sent in her direction by the pretty, pink-uniformed maids who served the meal. It wasn't until the coffee cups were being placed on the table that the truth dawned.

Rosa entered with Juan, who had been having his own lunch party with his friends in the kitchen, and came to give her a kiss before going upstairs for his *siesta*. Rosa's beaming face, as she contemplated Alexia and Rafael, echoed by those of the serving girls, made it plain that this morning's encounter between herself and Rafael was now the talk of the kitchen.

Alexia blushed and stared down at her cup, but not before she had caught a mocking glance from Rafael, who also appeared to have understood the situation.

The luncheon party broke up as Doña Maria and Juan went upstairs for their *siestas*, while the guests moved outside to where more coffee and liqueurs had been set out on small tables beneath a shady tree. Alexia, tired from her sleepless night and the dramatic events earlier in the morning, sank down on a comfortable chair, talking desultorily to Rafael's record producer.

Julia and Isabella disappeared into the house, leaving Michael and Rafael sitting together, buried deep in conversation. Not able to hear what they were saying, Alexia noted, with a vague sense of unease, the frequent speculative glances Rafael cast in her direction.

The girls came back laughing together into the garden, collecting Michael on their way to the pool. Rafael sat alone, in contemplative silence, studying Alexia fixedly from beneath his heavily hooded eyes, before getting up and walking over to sit down beside her.

'Well, well!' he murmured. 'I have just had an interesting talk with your friend Michael. He thinks very highly of your work with computers, very highly indeed. I didn't realise you were such a clever woman, Alexia.'

She flushed beneath the sardonic glitter of his dark eyes. 'I'm not particularly clever,' she said as firmly as she could. 'Most children in school grasp the concept immediately. Unfortunately, if you mention the word "computer", the general public goes glassy-eyed and has visions of robots marching down the High Street.'

'Michael tells me that you were originally a pupil of his at a technical college, where he lectured on computer technology and business studies, yes?'

'Yes.'

'He also tells me that you interrupted your studies and left, after only a year, because your sister—Antonia?—because she died, yes? So that when Michael decided to set up his own ... er ... software company, you began working for him and others, from your home.'

'Yes.'

'Why?'

'Because I needed the money, of course,' she snapped nervously.

Rafael sighed. 'Come now, my dear Alexia, you are being deliberately monosyllabic, and also deliberately obtuse. I am asking why you should have to leave your technical college when your sister died.'

'For purely private, family reasons,' she answered sharply, trying to still the nervously twisting hands in her lap. It's like that dreadful children's game of grandmother's footsteps, she thought in sudden panic. Ever since that meeting in Rafaél's hotel room, she had been trapped by the evasion, if not the downright lie, about Juan's parentage. He was sure to find out the whole miserable story very soon, she shivered nervously at the thought of his dreadful anger at having been decieved.

'You left your studies to look after your mother and father, yes?' he persisted, his intense gaze focused on the bowed head of the girl beside him.

'No. My father and mother were killed in a car crash when I was sixteen.'

'I am sorry,' he said quietly. 'I did not know that.'

Alexia raised her head and looked around the garden at the family and guests busily engaged in conversation, before turning back to Rafael. 'My dear man,' she muttered through clenched teeth, 'to quote your own words, "There are many things you do not know". From the first moment we met, in that ghastly cemetery, you've made many false and damaging assumptions about me. You wouldn't listen to the truth when I tried to explain it to you, in your suite in London. Oh no, you . . . you knew it all, didn't you?' She raised her coffee cup, staring grimly into his handsome face. 'You were quick enough to label me a "loose woman"—why this sudden obsessive interest in my past? As far as I'm concerned, my dear, oh-so-clever brother-in-law,' she hissed softly, 'you can go to hell!'

Rafael stared at her for a long moment, his eyes

blazing in a face suddenly gaunt and pale beneath his tan. Silently he rose and walked over to his guests.

'Please excuse me, everyone,' he said, 'but Alfonso, his colleague and I have much work to do. I hope you will stay and swim later,' he added, turning to Michael.

'Love to,' Michael replied promptly. 'I'll take Isabella home too, if that's convenient?' he said to the girl.

'Oh yes!' Isabella's eyes sparkled.

Alexia had looked at the animated girl with astonishment. In fact, she thought, Isabella had been remarkably vivacious throughout the visit. She noticed that Rafael also gave his fiancée a searching glance as he left the garden. I do hope Michael is careful, she thought. He may find Isabella attractive, but Rafael is unlikely to stand any nonsense there. 'What's mine is mine' is stamped all over his personality—and anything else he can lay his hands on, she thought bitterly, still shaken from her encounter with Rafael.

And that had been the last she had seen of him, before he had left for Madrid.

She was jerked back to the present by Juan's voice. Glancing up, she saw Doña Maria, looking cool and serene, examining the sandcastle under the eagle eye of its builder.

Alexia rose from the shade of the tree and walked over.

'May I please steal Juan for the rest of the day?' his grandmother pleaded. 'My best friend has asked me to tea. For years she has bored me with tales of her wonderful grandchildren, and I would so like to take my revenge!'

'Of course,' Alexia smiled. 'He's been working very hard on his sandcastle, so with any luck he won't be too boisterous and let you down in front of your friend.'

'Oh no, my dear. You've brought him up beautifully. He has lovely manners.' Doña Maria smiled warmly at the girl. 'You are very generous in letting me have so much of his time.'

'Oh no, I . . .'

'Yes, you are a lovely girl. It makes me very happy to have you here,' she said, giving Alexia a quick hug. 'You are very good for Rafael, too.'

'Oh no! I m-mean . . .' Alexia stuttered confusedly. 'I'm afraid Rafael and I . . . we—we don't get on very well. I mean . . . I'm afraid we . . . er . . . argue a lot . . .'

'Yes, so I understand!' Doña Maria's eyes twinkled.

Alexia blushed a deep crimson. Oh lord! she thought, Rosa's told her about it all as well!

'Nevertheless, you are very good for Rafael, very good indeed. He is my very dear son, but I have to admit that until only recently he had become very arrogant and frankly, my dear, very boring.'

'*Boring*? Mind you,' Alexia said grimly, 'I can think of a lot of other words for him, but boring certainly isn't one of them!'

Doña Maria laughed. 'No, he hasn't been boring lately, has he?' Still laughing, she took the little boy's hand. 'Come along, Juan, let's go for a ride in the car.'

Alexia looked after the retreating figures in puzzlement. What an extraordinary household! No one, not even his mother, seemed at all worried or upset that she and Rafael had been caught in a passionate embrace—despite the fact that he was engaged to be married. Maybe they were all mad? Certainly Rafael was. She shrugged helplessly and decided to have a swim.

Later, lying on her towel in the shade of a pine tree, she sleepily tried to work out why Rosa and Doña Maria should not have been furious about what had happened. It was all very strange . . .

Alexia came slowly back to consciousness. She must have fallen asleep, she thought bemusedly, as she rolled over and stretched out languidly.

A small sound made her turn her head, to find Rafael lying beside her on the sand. She gazed drowsily at him, as he lay sideways facing her with his head propped up on his bent arm.

'Hello,' he said, smiling gently. 'You were fast asleep, curled up like an elegant golden lioness, and I didn't want to wake you.'

She smiled mistily back at him, still half asleep. He looks wonderful, she thought idly, gazing at his broad shoulders and deeply tanned chest, where a gold chain nestled amongst the black curly hair. He was wearing a pair of pale blue swimming trunks and his long legs, the shade of mahogany, seemed to stretch for ever.

'Aren't you supposed to be in Madrid?' she said slowly, still not really awake, her heart beginning to beat uncomfortably fast.

'I flew back early, and I can see it was worth it!' His eyes roamed over her long, slim golden body, clad in a brief white bikini.

Alexia blushed under his gaze. She had got so used to her new swimwear that she had ceased to think about how little it concealed. Until now, that was.

She sat up hurriedly and began to pin up a tendril of her hair which had fallen from the knot on top of her head. Glancing sideways through her eyelashes, she caught a gleam from his eyes as they rested on her breasts, thrown into prominence by her action.

'What . . . what time it is?' she asked breathlessly,

suddenly remembering their encounter at the lunch party. Alexia flushed as she recollected her furious rejoinder to his probing questions, the flash of anger in his eyes followed by his abrupt departure. What . . . what could she possibly say to him now? Did he remember what they had said to each other, as clearly as she did? Maybe he had forgotten—she fervently hoped so.

'The time? I've absolutely no idea,' he said carelessly. 'Shall we go for a swim?'

She hesitated. 'Yes . . . all right.' Anything was better than sitting here under his disturbing gaze.

'Would you . . . er . . . be kind enough to put some oil on my back? The sun's very strong today and I'd hate to burn,' Rafael said blandly.

With skin that colour, she thought, you need oil like I need a hole in the head! However, it would be unnecessarily churlish to refuse his request, so she took the bottle and knelt behind him, silently beginning to spread the suntan lotion over his broad muscular back.

'What soft hands you have, Alexia,' he murmured, turning his head to smile at her.

'All the better to smack you with, and . . . and if you don't keep still, that's exactly what I'll do!' She grinned, a small nervous gurgle of laughter shaking her slim body at the recollection of the story of Red Riding Hood.

'Alexia! I had an English governess when I was small, and so I know exactly why you are laughing. Shame on you!'

'A Big Bad Wolf is exactly what you are!' she retorted wryly. 'There, I've finished, although both you and I know that you didn't really need any oil.'

'Ah yes, you are right, of course,' he turned around. 'But I did so enjoy it!'

'You're hopelessly incorrigible,' she told him severely, her hands trembling slightly as she tried to replace the cap on the bottle.

'Now it's my turn,' he said, the gleam in his eyes more pronounced then ever.

She got to her feet and backed nervously away. 'Oh no! I'm . . . I'm not falling for that one.'

'Falling for what?' he protested, his face a mask of hurt innocence, his eyes dancing with amusement.

'Come off it, Rafael. I may be a blonde, but . . . but I'm not dumb!'

He laughed. I promise you I will be very good. Without the oil you will burn—really you will.'

'No tricks?'

'No tricks—I promise.'

Still doubtful, she turned her back to him, shivering involuntarily as she felt his warm hands moving gently over her shoulders.

'Just to prove what a trustworthy gentleman I am,' he told her, 'I am going to give you fair warning to hold tightly to the front of your bikini. I have to undo your strap, otherwise you will have a white line across you back. O.K.?'

She sighed. 'Oh, all right.'

His hands released the catch and continued to move slowly down her back, sending deep ripples of pleasure coursing through her body. The heat of the day, the scent of the pine trees and the gentle slap of the sea on the sand, filled her with languor and drowsiness.

'Tell me about my brother, Alexia,' Rafael said softly.

'What do you want to know?'

'Did you love him?'

There was a long pause, as his hands continued to

caress her skin. Rafael and his family deserved to
know the truth. Whether he would believe her was
another matter. She couldn't stand any more scenes
with him ... she really couldn't. She'd try and
explain. Maybe ... maybe he would be understanding
...

'I ... I wasn't in love with your brother, Rafael. But
he ... he was a good man and I came to care deeply
about him—of course I did.'

'He ... he must have loved you very much?' His
hands ceased to move for an instant as he waited for
her answer.

'No ... I mean ... this is all very difficult. I ... I
hope he cared for me, too. Yes, I'm ... I'm sure he
did. He always said he was very grateful ...'

'Grateful?' he breathed harshly. 'Grateful for your
... your loving attention to his ... er ... needs?'

'Well, I ...' Alexia shook her head, bewildered by
his questions and the suppressed anger in his voice.

'Was he passionate? Did he love you with much
passion?' he demanded thickly, burying his face in her
hair, his hands moving erotically over his hips.

'Rafael, I ... I don't think you understand. It
wasn't like that ... Luis and I ... we didn't ...' she
gasped, feeling faint with desire from his sensual touch.

'*Te quiero, mi* Alexia, *te queridisima* ...' he
murmured huskily, his hands moving higher and
higher over her soft skin. She was powerless to resist
as he removed the bikini top from her trembling
hands, his fingers cupping the creamy fullness of her
breasts.

'Oh no! You ... you promised ...' she moaned
weakly as he turned her sideways in his arms.
Hungrily his mouth found hers, exploring her parted
lips, making them quiver in response. He groaned

pleadingly, his warm hands moving over her taut
breasts as she lay in his arms, aware of nothing except
the overwhelming and totally consuming passion he
always seemed able to evoke in her.

Slowly removing his lips, he gently stroked her face,
before taking the combs from her hair and shaking free
the thick curls. Murmuring soft endearments in
Spanish, he began to cover her face with brief
butterfly-soft kisses. As his ardour increased, he
moved his mouth over hers, deliberately tantalising
and playing with her lips, until they parted again with
an urgency as fierce as his own.

He laid her back on a towel, and his lovemaking
became more demanding, more urgent. Drowning in
some deep fathomless sea, Alexia desperately strove to
reach the surface. Her body seemed to be moving against
his of its own volition—despairingly she realised that
there was nothing she could do to prevent it.

'Please,' she gasped, 'please ... help me. Please
don't ... I ... can't stop. I ...' Totally beyond
control, she burst into an emotional storm of tears.

'Hush, Alexia ... hush!' Rafael whispered, cradling
her in his arms and rocking her gently to and fro as
though she were a small child. 'It's all right, my
darling. *Te quiero*. It's all right.'

The great racking sobs which shook her slim frame
gradually ceased as he wiped her eyes, smoothing the
damp tendrils of hair from her perspiring forehead.
'You are so beautiful. I ...' He gazed down into the
green, gold-flecked depths of her eyes, sighing deeply
as he clasped her to his chest.

Exhausted by her tears, she lay quiescent, oblivious
of everything except the warm musky scent of his
body and the strength of his strong arms about her.

'*Querida!*' he groaned thickly, his lips moving over

her hair. 'I . . . I'm sorry. I . . . I broke my promise to you, didn't I?' He looked down at the trembling girl. 'God knows what comes over me when I'm near you,' he sighed.

Slowly returning to reality, Alexia began to shake in reaction to her emotional outburst, becoming sharply aware that she was only wearing her bikini briefs.

'I . . . I must get dressed. I . . .'

'*Por Dios*! Forget your damn clothes—it's not important!' he cried harshly as he held her away from him, looking searchingly into her bewildered and unhappy eyes.

'Leave me alone . . . please!' she whispered, looking about her desperately for something to cover her nakedness.

'Alexia . . . I . . .'

Snatching up a towel, she twisted out from beneath his hands and scrambled to her feet. 'For God's sake leave . . . leave me alone,' she gasped, her teeth chattering with tension. 'You know . . . you know it's just l-lust . . . You don't even like me!'

'Not like you . . .? *Dios!*'

'You . . . you don't! When you're not trying to kiss me—you . . . you're simply horrid to me . . .'

'You stupid woman!' he shouted angrily.

'There you go again!' she cried, her eyes filling with tears.

Rafael took a deep breath, smiling wryly up at her quivering figure. 'Surely, surely it is obvious that I . . . I wish to make love to you, *querida*?'

Her stomach knotted with tension at the warm, caressing tone in his voice, her legs feeling so weak that she leant against the trunk of the pine tree for support. 'But . . . but you're engaged . . .'

'Don't be childish, Alexia!' he ground out savagely.

'What in the world has my engagement to Isabella got to do with how I feel about you?'

She turned away to hide the sudden shaft of pain which seared through her body at his cruel words, her hands trembling as she replaced her bikini top. Desperately she fought to control the tears which threatened to fall, yet again.

'You ... you're quite right, Rafael. I ... I must seem very silly and immature,' she stammered haltingly with her back still to him, brushing down the fine sand sticking to her body. Feeling somewhat calmer, she turned to face him. 'I do understand that it's just ... just a matter of sexual attraction, and I ... I'm not blaming you. I'm just as ... as guilty—if that's the right word. Let's face it,' she said bitterly, 'I'm just a pushover, aren't I? So ... so please, I beg of you, just leave me alone. Surely that's not too much to ask?'

'Holy mother of God, Alexia! Of course it's too much to ask—haven't you heard a word I've been saying?' He jumped up and grasped her shoulders, his fingers biting into her flesh.

'You can cut out the Spanish macho bit, for a start,' she replied coldly. 'I have indeed been listening to every word you've said. In essence, you are happily engaged to be married to a fabulously beautiful girl. However, you ... you feel quite free in the meantime to ... to indulge yourself with anything female which happens to strike your fancy, and that appears to be me—at the moment. Oh yes, I *comprende* only too well, Rafael. Indeed I do!'

'*Por Dios!*' he shouted angrily.

'*Por Dios* yourself!' she snarled back, wishing to wound him every bit as much as his words had hurt her. 'Can you deny that if ... if I'd been a free and easy woman, we wouldn't be making love, here on the

sand, this minute? Well . . . can you?' Rafael's face was
blank, his dark eyes burning into hers as she lashed
him with her tongue. 'Of course you can't! And I'm
not . . . not denying my part in this. I'll admit that I
haven't . . . haven't behaved at all well, either. Having
said that—I've said it all, right? A quick one-two on
the beach, and then back to your fiancée. Right again?
God knows what the two of you get up to . . .'

'What Isabella and I "get up to" does not concern
you,' he said in a quiet, hard voice.

'You're so right! It's none of my business what you
do. Why should I care? I . . . I just feel damn sorry for
the girl, that's all!'

'Have you finished?' he demanded roughly.

'No, I certainly haven't! You . . . you didn't like it
when I referred to your sexual appetite the other day,
but . . . but what else can I call it? Oozing charm, and
. . . and leaping on any available woman! You're like a
. . . a stag in rut!'

'*I'm what* . . .? Say that again, Alexia, and I'll . . . I'll
. . .' his face was dark with fury.

'You'll what? Don't try and threaten me!' Alexia
was by now past caring what she said. In some way
that she didn't understand, she was actually gaining a
perverse pleasure from torturing herself and Rafael.

'You've been perfectly foul to me, since the first
moment we met. So . . . so anything else you feel like
saying, or doing, is not going to make any difference.
Since it would seem that unlike normal men, one
lovely wife-to-be isn't enough for you, maybe you
ought to see a doctor. Perhaps he can give you
something to . . . to calm you down. The . . . the sort
of stuff my uncle once told me about. The—bromide,
I think it was—they used to put it in the Naafi tea
during the war. It apparently kept the troops' mind off

women . . . maybe it can do the same for you!'

Alexia stood glaring at him, her whole body rigid with fury. Then to her surprise his shoulders began to shake, and before her astounded gaze he started to laugh. Helplessly he shook his head at her, clasping his stomach in agony.

'Oh, Alexia!' he gasped, swept by another gale of laughter. 'N-Naafi t-tea!' he hooted, the tears running down his face, as he leant helplessly against a pine tree. '*Dios!*' he groaned as his mirth subsided, with only occasional barks of laughter breaking out now and then. 'Alexia—Alexia,' he smiled broadly, 'I've got to hand it to you. Your . . . your powers of invective are truly amazing. You may be a lot of things, my darling girl, but you are certainly not dull!'

'I'm not your darling girl,' she snapped sulkily, her fury beginning to subside a little. 'However, I . . . I suppose I was a . . . a bit rude,' she muttered, with a shrug of her shoulders.

'Another gracious apology from you, Alexia! In fact there is no need—I haven't had such a good laugh in years,' he said, wiping the tears from his cheeks.

'I'm glad you find it all so amusing!' she snapped angrily, picking up her clothes from the sand.

'*Un momento!*' he said in a hard, firm voice. 'I have taken a great deal of personal abuse from you. I do not intend to stand for any more nonsense—do you understand, Alexia?' He grasped her arm, his tall figure towering over her as he looked fiercely down into her apprehensive green eyes. 'For someone who is supposed to be so clever, you are behaving like a silly little girl. When we first met in London. I was—as you so graphically pointed out at lunch the other day—guilty of allowing previously formed ideas about your . . . er . . . past to cloud my judgment. Yes?'

'Yes, you wouldn't. . . .'

'I am,' he continued, blandly ignoring her interruption, 'still as confused about your past as ever, but I now know you well enough to know that you are not promiscuous—far from it.'

'Well, it's about time . . .' she muttered nervously.

'*Si!* And it is also about time,' he purred menacingly, 'that you stopped clinging so tenaciously to your first impressions about me, and the life I lead. Your crazy obsession about my sexual prowess would be laughable, if it wasn't so ridiculous!' He gave an angry bark of laughter, his hand tightening on her arms as he shook her in fury.

'Rafael, I . . .' she faltered, running her tongue over lips that were suddenly dry. Confused and exhausted by the emotional intensity of the past hour, she swayed wearily against his hard figure, the feel of his warm skin causing the blood to race through her veins.

'*Dios . . .!*' Rafael swore violently, gazing down into the green eyes clouding over with desire, the innocent provocation of her trembling soft lips. 'Enough, Alexia!' he groaned, pushing her roughly away, a pulse beating in his tightly clenched jaw. 'Go back to the house and leave me to swim,' he commanded harshly.

Alexia looked after his tall figure, striding purposefully towards the water, as she reached blindly for her towel and turned to walk back to the house with slow, hesitant footsteps.

Later that night, Alexia lay awake staring at the ceiling. It was no use . . . she really couldn't get to sleep. Sitting up, she put on her bedside light and saw that it was two o'clock in the morning. She sighed heavily. Maybe if she read for a bit, it might help. She looked around for the novel she had been reading earlier in the day, then frowning with annoyance, she realised that she had left it downstairs in the study. Oh well, she'd just have to go and fetch it, anything was better than lying awake in the dark until morning.

Returning from the beach, she had collected Juan from his grandmother and put him to bed, telling Rosa that she was very tired and intended to spend the rest of the evening in her room. She had lain in a hot bath, then sat by her window in the gathering dusk, staring blindly out at the sea, her thoughts in a turmoil. A turmoil with which she was still wrestling at this late hour.

Resolutely she swung her legs out of bed, not bothering to put on a wrap on such a hot night, tiptoeing along the corridor and down the stairs of the silent house. Feeling her way across the dark hall, she slowly opened the door of the study.

She was startled to see the light of the desk lamp glowing dimly in the large room and to hear soft music being played on the record player. It took her some moments to realise that Rafael was sitting with his back to her at the desk, his elbows bent, his head resting on his hands.

Dressed in black trousers and a black silk shirt, he blended into the darkness surrounding the small pool of light cast by the lamp. Alexia hesitated for a moment, before trying to leave quietly. Rafael must have heard a sound or felt a draught from the open door, as he spun swiftly around on his swivel chair.

'Did you want something?' he asked, his voice devoid of any expression.

'I . . . er . . . I just came down for my book. It's so hot I couldn't sleep, and . . .'

'Well, you'd better come in and get it,' he said in the same tone.

She went over and found her novel on the table

beside the desk where she had left it. Now she was closer, she could clearly hear the record to which Rafael had been listening. 'That's ... that's the saddest music I've ever heard,' she murmured as the melancholic, slow notes of a horn took up the mournful tune.

'It's by Ravel: *Pavane for a Dead Infanta.* I find it exactly suits my mood this evening,' he said heavily.

Looking searching down at him, Alexia could see lines of strain etching his face, which looked pale and drawn despite his tan.

'Are ... are you all right?' she asked, concerned. 'You ... you don't look at all well. Is there anything I can get you?'

He spun his chair round to face her. Alexia was leaning forward anxiously, her wide eyes large green pools of concern, her hair a golden cloud about her shoulders, the bodice of her black silk nightgown, a farewell present from Melanie, fulfilling its designer's wish of revealing most, if not all, of her full breasts.

Rafael's eyes devoured her silently for a moment. 'I'm quite all right,' he sighed deeply. 'Go back to bed, Alexia.'

She felt a sudden longing to take him in her arms and comfort him. To hold his head against her breast and tell him that everything—whatever the trouble—that everything was going to be all right.

'Oh, Rafael, are ... are you sure there's nothing I can give you? An aspirin or something ...?'

He gave a harsh laugh. 'No, you can't give me anything!' He spun his chair back to the desk. 'Go away, Alexia,' he said in a cold, expressionless voice. 'Goodnight, and please close the door on your way out,' he added firmly.

CHAPTER SEVEN

HER pillow damp with helpless tears, Alexia fell into an exhausted sleep, only to wake two hours later, as the first flush of dawn filled her room. She got out of bed, putting on a T-shirt and a pair of brief shorts, before going down to the deserted kitchen to make herself a pot of strong black coffee. Carrying the tray, she silently let herself out of the house and walked across the grass to the swimming pool.

The air was cool and fresh, filled with the song of birds greeting the early morning sun rising slowly over the mountains to the east. The dew still lay heavily on the lawn, the grass of which, so unlike that in Britain, tickled the soles of her bare feet with its raffia-like roughness.

Choosing a table in the shadow of a column at the far end of the pool, Alexia sat down on a chair and placing her feet on the seat of another, leaned back closing her eyes.

What was she to do? What could she possibly do, except try and get back to London as soon as possible? Back to the life she had led for the past four years, the daily routine of her work and caring for Juan, where life was predictable and wherein lay safety. Like a sick animal whose only wish is to crawl away to lie quietly in the dark, Alexia sat hunched miserably in her chair, her mind and body crying out for sanctuary. Anywhere! She'd go anywhere, just as long as it was as far away as possible from Rafael.

She sat up and with shaking hands poured herself a

cup of coffee. She had walked blindly back up the stairs to her room last night, her stunned mind struggling to assimilate the dreadful truth, which had struck her with such a blinding force. As she had looked at Rafael, hunched unhappily over his desk, she knew that she was in love with him. Deeply, intensely and irrevocably, in love with him.

Oh lord, what a mess! she moaned silently as she sipped the dark, strong liquid. Loving Rafael was, without a shadow of doubt, nothing but a one-way ticket to disaster! Not only was he engaged to that beautiful woman—her stomach knotted with tension at the thought—but he saw no reason why he shouldn't, at the same time, make love to Alexia. He's totally immoral, she thought with despair. How could she have been such a fool?

If only she had realised what was happening, maybe she could . . . well . . . have done something? If only she had led a normal life, as Melanie had so plainly pointed out, she might have had some idea of why she had always found him so disturbing. With more experience—any experience—she would surely have been able to recognise what was happening to her, taking avoiding and evasive action. You stupid, stupid fool! she cursed herself helplessly.

She sipped some more of the coffee as the sun rose, warming her long legs stretched out on the chair before her. It was too late, of course. She sighed deeply. Maybe it had always been too late. Even if she had realised, earlier on, that she was falling in love with Rafael, what could she have done?

Shivering nervously, she remembered the times he had held her in his arms, the feel of his warm hands on her body . . . the melting sweetness of his kisses . . . There was no going back, no place to hide. She was trapped, with no avenue of escape, trapped by her overwhelming love for Rafael.

It wasn't just a matter of passionate desire, which unsatisfied would eventually burn itself out. What she felt was a far deeper emotion. A need to care and comfort him, a desire to lie quietly in his arms, sheltered from the harsh winds of life. Oh yes, she was in love with him, all right . . .

This really won't do, she told herself firmly. You must try and pull yourself together. Whatever happens, you must make sure that he doesn't guess how you feel about him. She suddenly squirmed with embarrassment. She could imagine Rafael's lazy laugh if he ever found out. There was no way she was going to join the throng of women who so obviously adored him, none of whom made any secret of the fact that they would happily give their all, at the merest twitch of his little finger. *No way!* Despite what she had said on the beach, he seemed to believe that she had been in love with Luis. Well, let him believe so . . . it was much safer for her that way.

She glanced at her watch. It was time she went indoors and woke Juan. She had been so preoccupied with her feelings about Rafael that she was in danger of neglecting the poor little boy. She smiled wryly at her thoughts. The 'poor little boy' was having the time of his life, which was the only reason why she had to stay for the full month. Doña Maria was enjoying herself so much with her new grandson that Alexia really couldn't just selfishly pack up and leave.

'Up, Guards, and at 'em!' She remembered Rafael's quotation at the lunch party. Yes, she'd just have to face up to her problems and muddle through, somehow.

Feeling somewhat calmer than she had earlier on,

Alexia rose and walked to the edge of the pool surround, looking down over the cliff edge at the beach and the sea beyond. Suddenly her mind was in turmoil again as she saw Rafael on the sands below. He was pacing slowly along the water's edge, his hands clasped behind him, his head bowed in thought.

Alexia looked at the tall figure of the man she loved. He was wearing only a pair of pale, ragged shorts, the sun glinting off the gold chain on his bare chest as he turned and retraced his steps. All her tortured feelings of love and despair overwhelmed the girl, her eyes filling with tears as she turned and walked unsteadily back to the house.

There was a knock on her bedroom door and Alexia quickly wiped her eyes. She seemed unable to stop the stray tears from trickling down her cheeks, however much she tried. I've cried more since I've known this family, she thought with misery, then I've ever cried in my whole life.

'Come in,' she called.

'*Buenos dias*, my dear. I just came to see if you are feeling well. You didn't come down to dinner last night, or breakfast this morning.' Doña Maria looked at her daughter-in-law, standing by the window.

'I'm fine . . . just fine. Really.'

'No. Me, I do not think so.' She walked over to Alexia, gently touching a tear-stained cheek. 'I do not think so at all.'

'Doña Maria, I . . .'

'Come, I am having coffee in my sitting room. Please join me, yes?'

The older woman took her arm gently and, unresisting, Alexia allowed herself to be led to a sun-filled sitting room, bright with flowered curtains and glazed chintz-covered chairs.

'Now, you sit down, and I will pour us a nice cup of coffee. I drink it all day long, you know. My doctor says that it is not good for me, but . . .' Doña Maria continued to chatter, as she poured the coffee, deliberately not giving the girl a chance to say anything until the cup of hot liquid was in her hands.

The inconsequential words, washing over Alexia, had a soothing effect. She managed a tremulous smile of thanks as she shook her head at the proffered biscuits.

'My dear, I don't want to be a prying old woman, or a dragon of a mother-in-law, but if you would like to tell me what's wrong . . . Something is very wrong, is it not?'

'Doña Maria, I—I really . . .'

'Please call me Mamá, if you would like to. You see, you are my daughter now, if only by law. It would give me such pleasure.' She smiled sweetly at the unhappy girl.

'It would give me much pleasure, too . . . er . . . Mamá. Thank you.' She's so kind, thought Alexia, how could I possibly tell her what's happened to me? However, she has a right to know about Antonia and Luis . . . especially about her son Luis. 'I—I'm sorry if I seem a—a little upset. It's nothing at all, really.' She blew her nose determinedly. 'However . . . er . . . Mamá, something has been on my conscience, and I—I would like to talk to you about it.'

'Of course. It is also time we talked about Luis, is it not?'

'Yes, it's—it's about your son I . . .' she paused, trying to collect her thoughts. 'First of all, I have to tell you that a—a grave mistake has been made, and it's entirely my own fault. You see, when Rafael first met me ... at Luis's funeral ... he—he ...' she gulped, wiping her eyes.

'It's all right, my dear. Just take your time.'

'Well, I suppose it was understandable really. But he thought I—I was Antonia, and he said some things which I ... Well, I behaved very badly, and in a fit of temper let him think that I was her, and ...'

'Darling girl! I'm lost! Please, I don't understand any of what you are saying. Please can you start at the beginning?'

Alexia shook her head distractedly. 'Honestly, I don't know what's happened to me lately. I must be losing my mind,' she chastised herself. Sipping her coffee, she made a determined effort to be more articulate.

'The story begins with your son Luis and my sister Antonia. She was older than me and a very lovely girl ... really beautiful. Unfortunately, although it hurts me to say so, she was also very silly. The combination of good looks and a lack of plain common sense proved to be her undoing. She became the—the mistress of a really evil man, who ... er ... who made her "entertain" his friends and clients ... if you understand me?'

'Yes, I think so.'

'Well, she was shopping in a big London store one day and ... one of those silly things ... the lift got stuck and she and the other passenger, who was Luis, spent half an hour chatting to each other in the dark, before they were rescued. He was studying at the London School of Economics at the time and—well, that was that, really. He took her off for a drink, to celebrate getting out of the lift, and they fell in love.'

'That's very romantic. Very, very romantic!' Doña Maria smiled.

'I didn't know any of this at the time, of course. I had just finished school and about to go to the local technical college. Antonia told me all about it later.' Alexia paused to collect her thoughts.

'I did say that Antonia wasn't too bright—didn't I? Well, she really got herself into a muddle. She fell in love with Luis and they became ... became lovers. Unfortunately, she was still living with the other man and was frightened of telling Luis about her life with him. She thought Luis wouldn't love her if he found out, you see. At the same time, she was terrified of her "protector", who was a really bad man with criminal connections. The long and short of the matter is that when her "protector" went abroad on business, she left her expensive apartment and moved into Luis's small, pokey two-roomed flat ... and she never went back. She told Luis eventually. He had to know in the end, because the man had some of his thugs try to persuade her to go back.'

'*Oh, Dios!*' Doña Maria exclaimed in horror.

'I do wish I—I didn't have to tell you all these sordid details,' said Alexia, sorrowfully, 'but they are important to the story.'

'It's ... it's all right. I—I just felt so sorry for your sister.'

'That's generous of you, Mamá. It really is. Well, there were Antonia and Luis, really happy, I promise you; and then my sister found she was pregnant. The date of her conception was in doubt, you see. Luis, to his eternal credit, loved her so much that he didn't care who the baby's father was. However, Antonia did, and she was absolutely certain it was Luis's baby.'

'Of course ... I see. The baby was Juan ...?'

'Yes. You see, Antonia really did love Luis, very much indeed. So she refused to marry him until the baby was born, when she could prove to him, by blood tests, that the baby was really his. Or more precisely, not someone else's. Maybe they can tell by other means nowadays, but she didn't know any other way at the time.

'So, Juan was born. He did prove to be Luis's son and they should have lived happily ever after. Luis hadn't been feeling well the last few weeks before the birth, but he didn't want to worry Antonia. She, for her part, had an easy birth, insisting on leaving hospital forty-eight hours later. She was feeling well and lied to the doctors about having someone at home to help her. They just lived in a cheap little flat in Battersea, but they were so—so happy . . .'

Doña Maria fussed about, pouring another cup for them both, while Alexia wiped away the tears that were falling again.

'Thank you,' she whispered. Clearing her throat, she took up the sad tale. 'The rest of the story's awful, really. Luis had seen his doctor and was sent to the hospital for a day-long series of tests. Antonia began to haemorrhage soon after he left that morning and through a series of muddles—not anyone's fault really—didn't get taken to hospital until much later that day. The first I knew was a telephone call at my lodgings from my uncle, to say that she was not likely to live through the night.'

Alexia's face paled as she remembered her frantic drive through the dark London Streets to the hospital. 'Antonia did last the night and she talked to me, as much as she could. Then—then the next morning . . .' Alexia turned her sorrowing eyes to Luis's mother. 'Then—then she just slipped quietly away, dying in Luis's arms . . .'

'*Oh, la pobre mujer, mi cara* Alexia! Your poor sister!' Doña Maria was weeping openly.

Alexia swallowed, forcing herself to continue. 'Poor Luis collapsed. My uncle and I . . . we—we saw to everything. My uncle paid for someone to come and look after Juan . . . and then the next blow fell. This is going to be painful, Mamá, and if you don't want to . . .'

'No, no. Continue, Alexia, *por favor*.'

'It was about a month later. I had just finished my first year's exams, when I got a call from my uncle to come and see him at his office. He—he laid it straight down the line. Luis's doctors had confirmed that he had lymphoma, a cancer of the lymph glands. The prognosis was . . . well, it was bad. They held out no hope in the long term, although he might hope to have remissions from the illness. He would need a lot of treatment and be quite unable to hold down a job, or look after Juan. He would become progressively more weak and depressed, and . . .'

'My poor Luis!' moaned Doña Maria. 'First his Antonia, and then . . .'

'Someone had to look after him and Juan, and—and there was no one else but me, was there? I—I had promised Antonia, when we talked through the night in hospital, that I would look after Luis and the baby. I had given her my solemn vow to do everything that I could. My uncle . . . well, he's excessively Victorian, and he—he insisted that Luis and I were married. I was still stunned by the tragedy of losing my sister and hearing about poor Luis, so I—I just meekly agreed. I couldn't see what else to do . . .'

'Oh, my dear, dear girl! What a burden for you to carry! You were so young.'

Alexia shrugged. 'Not too young, Mamá. I was

nineteen. We got married quietly in the local register office and went home to look after the baby. It was as simple as that. Uncle Walter really was very good and gave us a small allowance which, with the help of the social workers, saw us through the first few months.'

'Alexia!' Doña María's eyes were full of tears. 'If only ... if only I had known! I could have done so much. *Por Dios. Por Dios!*'

'I wish I ... I'm so sorry that Luis never mentioned his family,' said Alexia. 'He seemed to withdraw into himself and—and after Antonia had died, he really had no wish to live. We ... our marriage was one of convenience only ... he never thought of anything or anyone except Antonia. I mean ... er ... we never ...'

'I understand, dear. You are trying to say that you didn't make love to each other, yes?'

Alexia nodded. 'When Juan was six months old, I went to see my uncle and borrowed a sum of money. With that I moved us into a better flat and spent the rest on a computer. I won't bother to go through all the ins and outs of building up my business, but I was successful and was able to look after Luis properly.'

'Was—was Luis in much pain?'

'No,' lied Alexia firmly. There was no need for his mother to torture herself with what was past help. 'No, he just grew weaker and weaker. I do want you to know that he had the best medical help I could buy. I promise you that I made sure he was as comfortable as possible. Towards the end, he grew so frail that he needed expert nursing around the clock. So I arranged for him to be in a really nice nursing home, around the corner from the new house I had rented six months before. Juan and I went to see him every day. He died very quietly and peacefully.'

'Oh, my darling, darling Alexia! How can I ever repay you for all you have done?'

'Please, I—I just wanted you to know that he didn't want for anything. I was sure you would need to know that.'

'Of course. I'm so grateful.' Luis's mother smiled mistily at the girl, her tears.

'The trouble was, as I said at the beginning, Rafael assumed, before he met me, that I was Antonia,' Alexia explained. 'Unfortunately, he—he made clear his opinion of her behaviour. If she hadn't been my sister, I might have agreed with him. But . . . well, we quarrelled very badly, and when he—he accused me of living off immoral earnings, I was so cross that I—I let him think I did!'

'Rafael? How could he think such a thing? That he should insult you so. *Dios!*'

'Please! It's mostly my fault. I was frightened of losing Juan, you see. Unfortunately he still thinks I'm Juan's mother, although I don't think that he . . . er . . . believes any longer than I'm a "lady of joy", or whatever they call them nowadays!' Alexia laughed weakly. 'I just felt I had to tell you the truth. You've been so good and kind to me that I—I've been feeling very badly about the deception. I'm only Juan's aunt and Rafael is his guardian, after all. I know I said some wild things to Rafael in the heat of the moment, but I would never stop Juan coming here. When he's older, I would be perfectly willing to let him go to school in Spain, if that's what you want.'

'I am never,' her mother-in-law said firmly, 'never going to be able to repay you, for all you have done and for the loving care you gave my son and grandson. Absolutely never!'

'It was just that I promised . . .'

'As for Rafael—he has behaved quite disgracefully! I am deeply ashamed of him. How could he ... *Es increíble!*' Doña Maria was clearly very angry.

'I—I did try to tell him, but by then it was too late. Please don't blame him, it's—it's all my fault.'

'Nonsense! Anyone can see you are a good girl. Anyone.' Doña Maria laughed softly. 'You are an extraordinary mixture, my dear. You are strong, capable and have known sorrow. But on the other hand, you never did seem to be a wife and mother of four years' standing. It has puzzled me, I must admit. Have no doubt that I shall talk to my son most severely ... most severely indeed!'

'Oh no!' cried Alexia anxiously. 'Please don't say anything. Oh—oh, please don't!'

'My dear, why ever not?'

'I—I don't want him to know. I can't explain, but please ... I do beg you not to saying anything. It's—it's all very complicated ...' her voice trailed unhappily away.

'Ah ...' there was a long pause as Doña Maria sat back in her chair, looking at the unhappy girl. '*Si, si.* Yes, I understand. But, my dear girl ...'

'I—I can't talk about it. Please—please don't say anything to Rafael ... anything at all. I—I would be most grateful if you didn't,' Alexia begged, her eyes filling with tears.

'It shall be as you say. I promise not to say a word.' The older woman rose and put her arms around Alexia, kissing her gently on the cheek. 'My son, he is very bad, very naughty ... full of prejudice. Dear girl, I do beg of you to beware of having too much pride ... Yes?'

Alexia looked at her with startled eyes, before resting her head against Doña Maria's shoulders, shaken by a storm of tears.

The older woman comforted her in silence, before drying her eyes. 'Come ... enough. Now, what are you going to wear for this masked ball my daughter Julia is so mad for?'

'Masked ball? I—I really haven't thought about it ...'

'Well, you must! The girls are going to make the masks tomorrow, so that is taken care of. But you must wear a long dress ... very grand. Have you such a one?'

'A ball gown? No—no, I haven't.'

'Good. We then have a perfect excuse to buy one, do we not? This has been a sad morning, let us cheer ourselves up and go out now, before lunch, and see what we can find. Yes?'

'Oh, Doña Maria ... Mamá, really, there's no need. I hadn't thought of going at all ...'

'Of course you are going! I insist on buying you a lovely dress. I will not hear otherwise. *Comprede usted?*'

Alexia laughed shakily. 'That you and Rafael are alike I—I *comprende* very clearly!'

'Of course!' Doña Maria joined in the girl's laughter. 'Only I am much fiercer, so you must just do as I say. We go now, yes?'

'Yes,' agreed Alexia, smiling. 'We go now.'

What a day, she thought, feeling somewhat dazed, as she hung her new dress in the cupboard. Doña Maria had summoned her driver and within a few minutes they were on their way to Marbella. Rafael's mother had known exactly which shop to go to and together they had chosen a truly wonderful ball gown. Alexia had paled at the price, but Doña Maria had insisted on paying, and that, as she was learning, was that! The older woman had also decided that they should have lunch in Marbella, ignoring Alexia's protests that she really ought to be getting back to Juan.

'With Rosa he is happy. Let us enjoy ourselves. Besides,' she added, flicking an imaginary crumb off the table, 'I have a feeling that you would not wish to attend a family lunch today.'

Alexia flushed, and hung her head.

'Yes,' Doña Maria smiled, 'we are having a day "out on the toot", as Rafael's English governess used to say!'

'Mamá . . . you have been so kind to me . . .'

'*Por que?* It is nothing to what you have done for my family. Nothing! Also, you are my only daughter-in-law and a good girl. It is my pleasure.'

Well, you'll soon have another daughter-in-law, thought Alexia gloomily. At that moment she thought she saw Isabella walking by on the other side of the road, with Michael. They were gone in a flash, and on reaching home later in the afternoon, she decided she had been mistaken, because Isabella was in the sitting room, waiting to see Rafael, who was out.

That girl with Michael really had looked like Isabella, but then most Spaniards are dark, thought Alexia, as she closed the cupboard door on her new, glamorous dress. She was feeling quite tired, hardly having slept at all last night. It might be an idea to have a short nap.

She went over to draw the curtains—and froze. Rafael and Isabella were walking down the lawn to the pool, deep in conversation, and it looked from her gestures, as if the Spanish girl was doing most of the talking. Alexia watched Rafael with misty eyes. The sight of his long, slim elegant figure brought a lump to her throat. She was just about to move away from the window, when she saw Rafael turn to his fiancée and throw back his head, roaring with happy laughter.

A cold knife twisted in her heart as she watched him clasp Isabella in his arms, kissing her passionately. Alexia gasped with pain, stumbling blindly across the room to throw herself down on the bed, her body racked with sobs.

I hate him, the double-dealing swine . . . I hate him! she raged silently as she wept. But of course she didn't . . . she couldn't fool herself. She loved him with all her heart.

'Another glass, Pedro. Keep 'em rolling!' Alexia laughed at the barman, nearly falling off her stool. She turned to Jerry who was mumbling something beside her. 'I'm . . . I'm sorry, Jerry, what did you say?'

'. . . so I said to her, what about the alimony? If you think I'm supporting that young lover of yours . . .' He gazed owlishly at Alexia as he watched the barman pour her another drink. 'Say, honey, don't you think you've had enough?'

'No, def-definitely not. We came out to drown our sorrows, didn't we?'

'Sure thing, kid. We certainly did.'

'Well then—we haven't drowned yet. Look . . . whee!' Alexia spun around on her stool.

'Yeah, you're definitely floating! I don't think you're used to hard liquor, honey.'

'No,' she said solemnly, 'I am not. But . . . but there comes a time in every girl's life when she feels like getting stinko—and tonight's the night! Come on, Pedro, you're falling behind on the job. *Mucho vino pronto!*'

'You're one hell of a girl, Alexia. I could really go for you.' Jerry put an arm around her shoulders.

'That's nice, Jerry. It . . . it really is,' she sniffed. 'But . . . but I've got more on my plate than I can handle at the moment. Let's just stay good pals?' She gave him a peck on the cheek. 'Now, go on telling me about your wife. Why don't you just tell her you love her, and want her back?'

'Like I said, honey, she really doesn't . . .'

Jerry continued with his sad tale of wifely desertion. His words failed to penetrate Alexia's consciousness, her mind being filled by her own unhappy thoughts, which were obstinately refusing to be anaesthetised by alcohol.

She had been woken by Rosa, early in the evening, telling her there was a telephone call for her, and to take it on the landing outside her room. Grabbing a dressing gown, she had staggered half asleep to the phone.

'Hi, Alexia?'

'Yes, Jerry? Is that you?'

'Sure thing. My God, trying to get hold of you is worse than trying to break into Fort Knox! I keep getting Rafael on the line, and he sure doesn't seem to like me any more. Anyway, kid, how about coming out for a meal tonight?'

She had been about to refuse, when she heard a faint click on the line. Rafael's listening in—the damn eavesdropper! she thought with fury. I'll show him! she fumed silently, fully awake by now.

'Oh, Jerry,' she said in as low and sexy a voice as she could manage, 'I'd really love that. It sounds,' she gave a throaty laugh, 'it sounds a great idea.'

'Well . . . er . . . great!' Jerry was clearly somewhat overwhelmed by the come-hither tone of her voice. 'Fantastic—I'll pick you up at half eight,' he said enthusiastically. ' 'Bye now.'

' 'Bye, sweetie,' she trilled, and heard with satisfaction Rafael slam down his receiver with a muttered oath, seconds after Jerry had replaced his.

Her fury had abated by the time she stood in front of her mirror, bitterly regretting having agreed to go out with Jerry. She really didn't feel like being bright and sparkling this evening, and as for the dress, she must have been mad to allow Melanie to persuade her to buy it—and absolutely out of her mind to even think of wearing it tonight.

Made of thin black chiffon, its full skirt was clasped tightly by a gold belt at the waist. The bodice, cut very low in a gold-edged V-shape, revealed the rising fullness of her unconfined breasts on either side of the opening.

Heavens, she thought with horror. I look absolutely indecent! One sight of me in this dress, and Rafael will only have his rotten ideas about me reconfirmed. Still, who cares about him anyway? I certainly don't!

Her brave thoughts didn't convince even her, and she decided to change and wear another dress. Glancing at the clock, she realised with a sinking heart that she had no time—Jerry's arrival was imminent. Shaking with apprehension, she left her bedroom and went downstairs.

The family were having drinks in the sitting room, and her entrance did not go unnoticed.

'Wow!' Julia exclaimed. 'That's a really fantastic dress.'

Doña Maria blinked slightly, while Rafael stood staring transfixed at Alexia as she went over to speak to Julia. His face darkened and he clenched his fists, before walking slowly over to the drinks tray. He brought her over a glass of wine, and stood looking grimly down at her. 'You are going out, I presume,' he said in a hard voice.

'Oh yes,' she said airily, her bland smile hiding the nervous trembling she felt inside. 'Didn't you know? I was sure you must have *heard*.'

Rafael's face flushed with anger and she thought he was going to explode, when they heard the door bell.

'Aha,' she said brightly, in a slightly hysterical voice. 'That will be Jerry. I must dash ...' and grabbing her shawl, she made good her escape.

'Whew!' she muttered, climbing into Jerry's large chauffeur-driven car with legs that trembled like jelly.

'My God! You look great!' Jerry goggled at her ensemble.

'Jerry, I ... I don't want you to get the wrong idea. Tonight I feel like ... like drowning my sorrows. Let's just have a quite meal and then hit the alcohol. O.K.?'

'Anything you say, kiddo,' he agreed. 'But make sure you keep that shawl on—real tight. I'm only human, you know! Drive on, José,' he told the driver.

Alexia came back to her surroundings, a miserable lump of despair settling in the pit of her stomach. No amount of alcohol, it seemed, could assuage her unhappy longing for Rafael's tender embrace.

Jerry was entertaining the other customers in the bar with a spirited rendering of 'My Darling Clementine.' Some of the words didn't sound quite right, she thought bemusedly, in fact they were downright rude. She suddenly felt the amount of drink she had consumed begin to rapidly catch up with her.

'Come on, honey, let's call it a day before you pass out—huh? I'll just call José, and we'll take you home.'

'Here we are,' cried Jerry, as his vehicle came to rest

outside the Valverde house. 'It takes Two to Tango
. . . Two to Tango . . .' he sang loudly, opening his
door. 'May I have this dance?'

'Sh-certainly you may,' laughed Alexia tumbling
out of the car. 'My . . . hck . . . pleasure!'

'No, dear lady,' he said, bowing low, 'entirely mine,
I ash-assure you!' and they fell against each other,
laughing weakly.

'If you two have quite finished . . .!' a hard voice
thundered from the porch, 'it is obviously time Alexia
went to bed.'

'Oh, look!' she cried, twirling around. 'If it isn't old
Rafael . . . the man I love to hate! Hello, darling,' she
waved, 'we've had such a lovely time . . . haven't we,
Jerry?'

'Absh-absolutely!' Jerry replied. 'I will now leave
this lovely little girl in your capable handsh, old pal,'
he hiccuped, weaving his way back to his car.

'But, Rafael, I haven't had a dance,' laughed Alexia,
as his firm hand closed over her wrist and he led her
purposefully towards the porch. 'It takes Two to
Tango . . .' she sang as she stumbled into the hall.

'You are drunk, Alexia!' Rafael looked angrily down
at her.

'Yes, I know,' she smiled happily up at him. 'For
the f-first time in my l-life. It's sh-lovely!'

'You won't find it so lovely in the morning!' his lips
twitched. 'What have you been doing all evening?'

'Aha! Wouldn't you like to know!' she giggled. 'Up
to no good, of course; that's what you always think—
isn't it? Actually,' she confided, 'I decided to look sexy
and drown my sorrows in the demon drink.' She
jerked her arm from his grasp and spun around in a
circle. 'Do you think I look sexy, Rafael?' she asked
with a mischievous smile.

'Yes,' he replied shortly. 'Come on Alexia. It's time you went to bed.'

'Oh, I do feel . . . feel dizzy. Rafael, I . . . I don't feel very well,' she said in a small voice.

'*Dios!*' He swept her up in his arms, carrying her swiftly upstairs to her room, depositing her on the bed. He stood looking down at her with a frown. 'You are going to have a very bad head in the morning. Get undressed and I'll go and get you something which might help.'

He returned with a glass, to find Alexia still dressed and clinging to the frame of the bathroom door, her face pale and wan.

'Oh, Rafael,' she whimpered, 'I've been so sick!'

He smiled wryly. 'I'm not surprised. Come and drink this.'

'I . . . I daren't move the whole room is going around and around . . .' she whispered in distress.

'Oh, my Alexia,' he gave a dry bark of laughter. 'The wages of sin!'

'Don't laugh—please help me,' she pleaded. He sighed and holding her tightly, helped her to the bed. Sitting down beside her, he put an arm about her shoulders, and placed the glass in her trembling hands.

'Drink up,' he said bracingly, as with a shudder she emptied the glass.

'Ugh—that was awful!' She turned to lean against his shoulder, gazing up into his handsome face which was smiling gently down at her.

'Let that be a lesson to you,' he said softly as he stroked her hair. 'It is not good to drink too much, and certainly not for a woman.'

She yawned. 'I know, I'm sorry. I'll never, never do it again. It was just that I was . . .' she yawned again,

'. . . was so very unhappy. . . .' Her arms stole up around his neck. She sighed with contentment as she closed her eyes and nestling against him, she fell fast asleep.

'Oh, Alexia,' Rafael laughed softly. 'Wake up! You must get undressed and go to bed.' But she was totally unconscious, her only response to his voice being to snuggle closer to him.

'Alexia,' he told the sleeping girl, gently unwinding her arms from his neck, 'you'll never forgive me for this, but I can see no alternative!' He laid her down on the bed and swiftly undressed her, before rolling her nude body between the cool sheets.

'Alpha-plus for self control, Rafael,' he muttered wryly to himself as he pulled the sheets up over her shoulders, before kissing her forehead and leaving the room.

'Come on, it's time for breakfast.' Alexia slowly opened her eyes and saw Juan tugging at the bedclothes.

'Oh!' she groaned. 'Juan, just give me a moment to . . . Oh!' She sat up gingerly, holding her throbbing head. Carefully, very carefully, she lifted her wrist and squinted down at her watch. It was indeed time for breakfast. There was no help for it, she would have to get up.

'I'm . . . I'm just going to have a shower, Juan. I've got a shocking headache. Go and . . . er . . . play with your bricks—I won't be long.'

'Hurry up—I'm hungry,' he said, going off to get his bag of bricks, which he dragged into her room. 'I'm going to build a castle here,' he announced.

'All right,' she said abstractedly, glancing down at her nude body which should, by rights, have been wearing a nightgown. Why was she wearing nothing? She began to blush a deep crimson as scattered memories of last night came flooding back.

Stepping cautiously out of bed, she walked slowly and carefully to the bathroom and stood beneath a tepid shower. Her sluggish wits were refusing to remember more than the fact of being sick, and then drinking some foul liquid given to her by Rafael. After that . . . nothing!

What had happened? Various suggestions, all of them acutely embarrassing, flitted through her sore head. She let the water stream over her hair and body, as she cudgelled her brains. But try as she would, she could remember nothing more.

Her mind was suddenly filled with the image of Rafael and Isabella embracing yesterday, out by the pool. They had both looked so happy, it seemed as if they would soon get married, she tortured herself. She must try and leave sooner than the month allotted for her holiday. Maybe Michael could help her to manufacture some excuse, some pressing work, which would necessitate her departure for England.

She slipped into a simple jade green sundress, and tying her hair with a bow at the back of her neck, she took Juan's hand, bracing herself to go downstairs.

'Alexia's got a shocking headache,' Juan loudly informed the family as they entered the dining room.

There was a concerted murmur of sympathy from Julia and Doña Maria, only Rafael, who had risen at her entrance, was silent. She glanced at him and blushed as she caught the amused sparkle in his eyes.

Oh lord! she thought in misery. Maybe he . . . maybe we . . . did.

'Just a cup of tea, please,' she said in a low voice, in reply to Doña Maria's enquiry, and spent the rest of the meal wrapped in her own unhappy thoughts.

Julia left the table to go riding, and her mother took Juan with her to the kitchen to see the cook about lunch. There was a long silence as Alexia stared fixedly at her cup, aware of Rafael's steady gaze.

Eventually she plucked up enough courage to ask the question which occupied her thoughts to the exclusion of all else. 'Er ... Rafael,' she said, still looking down at the table. 'I ... er ... I don't remember much about last night, but ... did ... I mean ... did we ...?' Her voice trailed away, and she looked up startled as he began to laugh.

'Oh, Alexia, what a compliment! I do hope that when I make love to you, you will at least remember the occasion!'

She winced at both his words and his laughter, which seemed unnaturally loud. 'I didn't think anything like that,' she protested, then sagged as her head began throbbing again.

With her hand over her eyes—the light seemed very bright this morning—she admitted defeat. 'Yes ... well, I did wonder. You see, I ... I woke up with no clothes on,' she moaned.

'Yes, I know.'

Alexia flinched at the amusement in his voice. 'Rafael, I ... I feel like death warmed up. Please ... please don't be so ... so unkind. Just tell me what happened. I can't remember a thing!'

'My poor girl,' he said, his voice softening. 'It's really quite simple. I gave you some soluble aspirin and you promptly went to sleep in my arms. What was I to do? I couldn't leave you like that, for either Juan or the servants to see in the morning.' He got up from the table. 'What you need now,' he said, pouring some liquid into a glass on the sideboard, 'is a small brandy.

Force it down, and you may yet return to the land of the living!'

'Oh, I couldn't! I never want to see or drink alcohol again,' she shuddered.

'Very admirable. But you will find you feel much better with this inside you. Come on,' he put the glass before her, 'drink up!'

'Don't . . . don't bully me!' she moaned.

He laughed, and sliding his hand beneath her hair, began to gently stroke the back of her neck. 'All right. Please, dear Alexia, do me the favour—*por favor* . . .'

Her skin shivered at his touch as she stretched out a shaking hand for the glass, tipping the fiery liquid down her throat.

'That's a good girl. You will feel much better very soon.' He pulled up a chair and sat down beside her.

She glanced fleetingly at him through her eyelashes. 'Did you really? I mean . . .'

'Did I undress you? Yes, I did.'

'Oh!'

Rafael reached forward and took both her hands in his, turning her sideways to face him. 'I have told you why I did it. My dear, I have seen the nude female form before, you know.'

'I just bet you have!' she muttered bitterly.

'Alexia!' he sighed, gazing at the girl's bent head. He put out a hand and gently tilted her chin up towards him. 'It was late and you were fast asleep. I undressed you as quickly as I could, with no ulterior motive except to help you. Please understand.'

Looking up into his grave eyes, she blushed and nodded. 'Yes, I . . . thank you.'

'Mind you, in the face of such temptation, I did think of awarding myself the Purple Heart for valour!' His wide smile hit her like a blow to the solar plexus, and she was suddenly breathless, as his hooded eyes gleamed down at her.

'I have much I wish to say to you, but I will wait until you feel better. However, please rest assured that when I make love to you, I shall make very certain that you are wide awake!'

She gasped at his effrontery, and tried to jerk away her chin from his unyielding hand.

'Leave me alone, you horrible man! I ... I don't want you to make love to me!' she cried, shutting her eyes as the throbbing in her head intensified.

'Oh yes, you do,' he said with maddening certainty, standing up and drawing her into his arms.

'My God, you're ... you're an arrogant bastard!' Trapped by his embrace, she glanced angrily up at him, infuriated by his laughing eyes and his certain knowledge of his attraction for her. 'I ... I know you think you're God's gift to women, but ... but I ... I just don't happen to fancy Spanish men.'

There was a long pause. 'But, my dear Alexia, you married one, did you not?' he drawled softly.

Feeling as though she had been suddenly hit with a sandbag, she looked up at him with dazed eyes. Not "fancying Spanish men" had been a feeble evasion, as they both knew. However, it seemed as if in trying to get out of the frying pan, she was about to fall flat on her face in the fire.

'You were married for over four years and had a child. One does suppose a certain amount of ... er ... passionate involvement with one Spanish man, at least. Hmm?' His searching glance and the silky tone of his voice warned her of dangerous quicksands ahead. 'Now, I know you are a passionate woman, Alexia. I really do. Your response to my lovemaking has been ... er ... entrancing! And yet ...' he looked down into her gold-flecked, green eyes, 'and yet there is something strange, something not quite . . .'

Oh lord, he's going to guess the truth in a minute, she thought in a panic. For the first time in her life she resorted to feminine wiles—and burst into tears. 'I don't feel well,' she moaned, and that was certainly no lie, she told herself. She felt dreadful.

'Ah, *querida*, I'm sorry to be so horrid to you.' Rafael bent to kiss her gently on the lips.

Forcing herself not to respond, she wriggled free of his arms. 'When . . . when I was talking of Spanish men, I . . . I was referring primarily to you, not Luis. You . . . you might find it impossible to believe—your conceit is so monumental—but frankly,' she took a deep breath, 'frankly you're not my style at all. I prefer my men more . . . more . . .' she waved her hand in a careless gesture.

'Oh, yes?' queried Rafael, his composure infuriatingly undented. 'Just how do you prefer your men, Alexia?'

'I . . . er . . . I've certainly no intention of discussing such . . . such intimate details with you, Rafael,' she snapped crossly. 'And . . . and certainly not first thing in the morning. We've only just had breakfast, for heaven's sake! In fact, I think you're becoming a . . . a raving bore!'

'Do you, *querida*? We shall see!' he laughed, blowing her a kiss as he left the room.

CHAPTER EIGHT

ALEXIA ground her teeth with frustration. Not only was Rafael impossibly conceited and arrogant—she loved him, damn it! Sighing deeply, she moved over to the table to pour herself some coffee, before sitting down and resting her chin on the palm of her hand. I've got to get away somehow, she thought in despair. I really have. Not only was Rafael bound, sooner or later, to discover the truth about her marriage to Luis, but she was sure to betray how she felt about him as well.

At the moment he was convinced, rightly, that she found him attractive. She shuddered at the thought of how he would react if he knew she loved him. He was arrogantly sure of himself quite enough already. He'd be impossible if he really knew how much she cared. She would have no defences against him—no defences at all.

Her wandering, chaotic thoughts were interrupted by Julia, who tumbled into the room with her usual vivacity.

'Come on up to my room, Alexia. Isabella has arrived with the masks she has made and we must try them on. Tonight's going to be such fun!'

'Masks? Tonight?'

'You can't have forgotten? We're all going to the masked ball. Mamá has invited lots of people around here for drinks first. I simply can't wait!'

'Gracious, I did forget.' Alexia looked at Julia doubtfully. 'I really don't feel . . .'

'Rafael says it's only a headache, and you'll feel better soon. Come on!'

'Your brother . . .' Alexia began wrathfully as she slowly got up from the table.

'Yes—he's awful, isn't he? Really callous . . . and I told him so. Still, I expect he's right, he usually is,' Julia laughed.

'That's the trouble. He's so used to getting his own way that he can't believe other people might have opinions of their own,' Alexia fumed.

'Don't you like him?' Julia looked concerned.

'Yes . . . er . . . of course I do,' she quickly reassured Rafael's sister. 'Only there are times when I could cheerfully throttle him!' She smiled, suddenly feeling much better. The dreadful man had been right about the brandy as well.

'He's a real softie underneath, you know,' Julia confided, as they climbed the stairs to her room. 'He gets terribly fierce with me sometimes, but I can always twist him around my little finger,' she added complacently.

'Julia,' Alexia smiled, 'you're every bit as bad as he is!'

Julia giggled as she opened the door of her bedroom.

'*Buenos dias,*' said Isabella, smiling up from the table in the middle of the room, which was covered with pieces of material. 'Have you come to help me with the masks?'

'Pressganged is the word, I think.' Alexia, inwardly nervous, smiled shyly at Rafael's fiancée, who was looking cool and lovely, as usual.

'Look what she's made for me,' said Julia, going over to the table. 'Isn't it lovely?' She held up the mask to her face. Made of blue satin, the mask had tiny blue feathers at the sides where it met her temples. 'It exactly matches my dress. Isn't Isabella clever.'

'Did you really make that?' asked Alexia in amazement. 'It's really lovely, and Julia looks super.' She regarded Isabella's beautiful face with depression.

Isabella shrugged modestly. 'It isn't difficult if you like sewing, which I do. Although I did try and persuade Julia that the feathers were—what is the expression?—a "bit over the top",' she smiled broadly.

'Oh, poof! I shan't take any notice of you two old hags,' the teenager grinned, sticking out her tongue at Alexia and Isabella. 'I think the feathers are beautiful, and for once I intend to outshine Isabella!'

'Well, this "old hag" thinks you don't have a hope,' Alexia said wryly as she drew a chair up to the table. 'What can I do to help? I give you fair warning that I'm no good with a needle.'

Isabella smiled. 'There is really not much sewing involved. I have already made the basic masks, it is just a matter of what shade of material you would like.'

'Heavens, I don't have a clue,' said Alexia, looking at the rainbow collection in front of her. Not only was Isabella a raving beauty, she could sew like an angel as well. Alexia sighed with despair at such perfection.

'What colour is your dress? We can maybe start from there.'

'Let's see?' Alexia turned over the scraps of material. 'It's ivory lace with an underskirt of emerald green, a greenier-green than the dress I'm wearing. Here, this is the colour.' She held up a piece of satin.

'*Bueno*! That is decided. An emerald green mask it shall be.' Isabella smiled and put her head on one side, as she considered the slim English girl before her.

'You have the most lovely hair. How are you going

to wear it? It is important,' Isabella explained, 'because the mask must be tied on somehow.'

'I honestly haven't given it a thought,' Alexia confessed. 'I really hate my hair. I expect I'll wear it up in a knot on top of my head. I usually do.'

Isabella looked at Alexia's long golden curls, loosely gathered back into a large bow at the back of her neck. 'I have an idea . . . may I show you?'

Alexia shrugged, allowing herself to be led to Julia's dressing table. Untying the bow, Isabella brushed the long, thick tresses back from her forehead and scooping up the hair from each side of her face, caught and fastened it behind, at the top of her head.

'Isabella! I can't wear it that way, I look about sixteen!'

'You look beautiful, Alexia,' she smiled. 'Really beautiful. How I wish I had hair like yours. The colour . . . *que hermosa!*'

'You're joking!' Alexia looked in the mirror at the Spanish girl standing behind her. 'I've never seen anyone as lovely as you. I mean it,' she said with emphasis, 'you're really outstanding.'

'I'm going to leave you two old "ugly sisters" to admire yourselves,' laughed Julia. 'Little Cinderella here has to go shopping for Mamá. *Adios!*'

Isabella and Alexia looked at each other in the mirror and burst out laughing. Julia left the room with a flounce, nearly colliding with Rosa, who was entering with a tray containing a jug of fresh orange juice. Rosa beamed at the girls, chatting in Spanish to Isabella before leaving the room.

Alexia lifted an eyebrow. 'What was all that about?'

'She said that it was good to see that we are friends.'

Alexia coloured slightly. 'I—I very much hope so, Isabella,' she said, surprised to find how much she liked the girl. 'After all, we are going to be sisters-in-law. When I bring Juan over for the holidays, as I have promised Doña Maria, it will be so nice to have someone here that I know, as a friend.'

Isabella looked flustered, and it seemed for a moment as if she was going to say something. She turned aside, however, busily pouring the orange juice into the two glasses on the tray.

'I mean,' Alexia strove to explain in the face of the girl's silence, 'it's all been very strange here, for me. I don't really know anyone. Meeting Michael has been a help, of course.' She smiled. 'I sound very insular, don't I? I'll be calling for fish and chips next!'

'Michael . . . he is very nice.' Isabella's lovely face blushed and her eyes sparkled. 'He is so handsome . . . in the English style. Yes?'

'Well, yes,' agreed Alexia slowly. 'I hadn't really thought about it, but yes, I suppose he is handsome, in a blond, blue-eyed way. How strange,' she added, 'I've known him for ages and I've never really thought about it. Yes, I suppose he is an attractive man.'

'Oh yes,' breathed Isabella, smiling broadly. 'Oh yes, he is!'

'Isabella!' Alexia looked at her startled. 'You're not . . . you can't . . . you're engaged to Rafael!'

'I love Michael,' the Spanish girl said simply, her eyes glowing. 'I love him very much.'

'But you can't! You've only known each other for a few days.'

'Time is not important, Alexia. We love each other, truly. Ever since that meeting in the Orange Square . . . I knew at once that he was the only man for me.' She leant over and squeezed Alexia's hand. 'We owe it all to you.'

'*Me?*' cried Alexia, looking at her in horror. 'For

God's sake, don't place it at my door! Rafael will be furious enough when he finds out. If he thought I had anything to do with it ... he'd—he'd ... Heaven knows what he'd do!' She shuddered at the thought of the cataclysmic row which she was convinced was about to shake the family home to its foundations.

'No, no,' laughed Isabella happily, 'all will be well.'

'I'm glad you think so. Frankly, I very much doubt it!' Alexia said gloomily.

'Oh yes. Michael is seeing my father today. All is well.'

The girl's on cloud nine, thought Alexia. If she says 'all is well' once more I'll—I'll kill her! All is very far from well. Poor Rafael, how upset he's going to be. I know it serves him right, but ... Her heart bled for the man she loved.

'Rafael's going to blame me ... I just know he is,' she sighed unhappily. 'Look, Isabella, are you sure you aren't making a mistake? You know ... a sudden attraction, a—a quick rush of blood to the head. It can happen.'

'*Absolutamente no!* I know for certain that it is Michael I love. I was never in love with Rafael ... or he with me.'

'*What?*'

'It is not unusual. Our fathers were good friends, I have known Rafael since I was a little girl. My father wished it ... and I didn't dislike Rafael; so ...' Isabella shrugged.

'... didn't dislike him?' asked Alexia, looking at her in bewilderment.

'You must understand. I know him too well, he is like a brother to me. There is no ...' Isabella hunted for the right words. 'There is no spark. He is nice, and kind, but ...' she shook her head. 'We find each other very boring, really we do. Now with Michael, it is very exciting, and he loves me. There are lots of sparks, yes?'

'Well, I suppose there's many kinds of love. Rafael does care for you, though, surely?'

'My papa is his godfather and Rafael is very fond of him. He respects him. When Papa spoke about our marriage, Rafael agreed. But truly, I believe the most important thing for him, was that our engagement meant the women left him alone. Well, some of them!' the Spanish girl laughed. 'It is truly amazing how the women fall for him. Amazing!'

Alexia coloured slightly, and sipped her drink. 'I—I do beg of you to reconsider, Isabella. Rafael will go bananas!'

'Bananas? I do not understand.'

'Sorry . . . it's slang for furious, angry, like a raging bull . . . you get the message?'

'No,' Isabella laughed merrily. 'He is very happy, very relieved . . . truly.'

'Happy? Relieved?' Alexia stared at Isabella, open-mouthed.

'Oh yes . . . I told him yesterday.' Isabella hummed happily as she sewed.

Alexia, her mind in turmoil, sat looking at the girl in a daze. 'I—I don't understand . . .'

'Rafael is a Spanish gentleman and he had given his word to my papa, had he not? If I had not told him I wished to cease our engagement, he would have married me, even though he did not love me.' She looked at the English girl, who did not seem to understand. 'It is very simple, Alexia. He had promised to marry me. He could not, *with honour*, go back on his word. A man's honour is very important in Spain.'

'I—I still find it difficult to—to believe that he's happy about you and Michael. I—I would have thought that he would be very possessive about you.'

'I must tell you, Alexia,' confided Isabella, 'that I was a little worried about telling him. But he was so grateful and happy, I could hardly believe it. He thanked me over and over again. I do think, don't you, that he should have been unhappy. It was not very nice for him to show such relief!'

Alexia started to laugh, a little hysterically. 'Isabella, how feminine! You change fiancés at the drop of a hat and then are chagrined to find Rafael isn't tearing his hair out!'

The Spanish girl grinned back at Alexia. 'It is silly of me, no? Rafael said he did not wish to marry, which is something I can understand. He said he wished to go free, for his singing. As he said, there is no time in his life for a permanent woman. It is a hard life, always travelling and staying in hotels.'

Alexia, whose heart had begun to flutter uncontrollably at Isabella's news, suddenly felt flat and depressed. Rafael was right, of course. A pop star's life was hardly an enviable one. Despite the broken engagement, everything was as it had always been.

'Here you are,' Isabella held up the mask. It was covered in green satin, and she had sewn tiny seed pearls on the winged sides.

'It's lovely . . . it really is,' Alexia tried to sound enthusiastic. 'You've made it beautifully, thank you so much. I—I hope you will be very happy with Michael,' she added.

'Yes, I shall be.' The girl smiled happily. 'Rafael didn't want me to say anything until he and Michael have talked to my papa. But I know you will understand. I had to tell someone, I really did! Even

Julia doesn't know yet, although I expect he has told his mother.'

'I won't say anything,' promised Alexia. 'I . . . er . . . I'd better go and see to Juan, I expect he's turned the whole house upside down by now.' She smiled wanly at Isabella, before walking slowly out of the room.

Alexia's entrance into the sitting room, later that evening, caused a sensation.

She had styled her hair as Isabella had suggested, and the thick golden mane rippled down the back of her bare shoulders, which rose from a deep frill of ivory lace, finely edged in emerald satin. A wide satin cummerbund in the same colour grasped her slim waist. Finely gathered ivory lace lay like a delicate cobweb over the crinoline skirt, caught up here and there with small bows, to display the emerald satin below.

The bodice was cut very low and she had decided to wear a choker of pearls, in an attempt to minimise what she felt was a bare expanse of flesh. She was innocently unaware that it merely served to draw attention to the rising fullness of her creamy breasts, while the green mask added a flavour of mystery to her beauty.

'*Señora*,' cried Alfonso, hurrying over to her, 'you look ravishing! *Deliciosa!*' There was a murmur of agreement from the guests, some of whom she had not met before. Several of the men cleared their throats and straightened their bow ties, in an unconscious tribute to her beauty.

Alexia blushed and smiled at Alfonso. 'It is only this lovely dress, which was given to me by Doña Maria,' she smiled at her mother-in-law, who had come up to give her a kiss of appreciation.

'Nonsense, Alexia! It is you who grace the dress.' Doña Maria smiled and turned to address the rest of her guests. 'Come, it is time we left. Rosa has just told me that Rafael has been delayed and will join us later.' She turned to Alexia. 'Apparently he is busy with a long telephone call from London. We will not wait for him,' she confided.

The nightclub was a revelation. Alexia had expected it would be small and dark, as she had supposed such places usually were. Instead it had large, vaulted rooms and a wide terrace overlooking the sea, lit by fairy lights.

Their party forced a way through the throng to where Michael and Isabella were already sitting among the seats reserved for Rafael's guests. Isabella, dressed in a shade of deep pink, looked ravishing, while Michael, in common with the other men, wore a white tuxedo and black bow tie.

'Hi,' he greeted Alexia, with a kiss on the cheek. 'You look simply lovely!'

'So does your . . . er . . . new fiancée,' she smiled at him.

'Shush!' he grinned. 'It's supposed to be a secret.'

'Honestly, you've got a nerve! It could have been very nasty. I'm still not convinced . . .'

'Look,' he said, glancing around, 'let's dance, we can talk more privately that way.

'What aren't you convinced about?' he queried, as they slowly swayed to the music.

'What do you think? Rafael, of course! Isabella says he's pleased, which doesn't sound a bit like him at all. I still have a ghastly feeling that life is about to become very grim for all of us.'

'Sorry about that . . . but all's fair in love and war! He was positively neglecting that poor girl. Can you imagine anyone not being mad about her?'

'No, I—I can't. You're right.'

'If he didn't have all those women . . . well, I might think . . .'

'You'd be wrong!' Alexia retorted sharply, colouring under his surprised gaze.

'Ho, ho! So that's the way the wind lies, does it?'

'No, it doesn't,' she said crossly. 'But he can't help trying to keep his hand in . . . when he gets the chance. Which he—he doesn't,' she added hurriedly. 'Not— not with me anyway.'

'O.K., I get the message. Anyway, we owe it all to you. If we hadn't met that day in Marbella . . .'

'Thank you very much!' she said dryly. 'Rafael's going to be really grateful to me, isn't he?'

'Oh, stop worrying about him. Apparently he's happy to be footloose and fancy-free. So who cares?'

I do, for one, she thought, a heavy weight of depression suddenly descending on her slim shoulders. She sighed and tried to concentrate on the throng of people around them.

'Some of the masks people are wearing are really fantastic,' she said, looking around. 'There's one over there that . . . Oh!' she gasped, as she saw Rafael at the top of the stairs which led down to the main room.

He stood in the doorway, immaculately dressed in his evening ensemble with a plain black mask over his eyes. She would, of course, have known him anywhere, but she did not know the two blonde girls on either side of him, clinging to his arms and looking up with adoration into his face.

He casually surveyed the dance floor beneath him, his gaze passing over Alexia as if he had never seen her before, although she was certain she had caught a brief glint from his masked eyes as they swept over her and Michael.

The motion of the dance prevented her from seeing any more, and when she looked up again, the top of the staircase was empty.

'Let's explore this place,' Michael suggested when the music stopped.

'What about Isabella? Won't she . . .'

'Frankly, Alexia, Rafael's just come in. For the moment I've decided that discretion is definitely the better part of valour!'

'What a rotten coward you are,' she grinned.

'You're so right! Come on, let's disappear for a bit.'

When they returned to the table some time later, Alexia was immediately claimed by Alfonso who reluctantly yielded his place, after a dance, to another of the guests.

'I insist on taking you into supper,' he said. 'Don't forget now!'

'I won't,' she promised, as the band struck up again. Maybe the people present that night were more used to a nightclub shuffle, but she and her partner were the only dancers on the floor as they whirled and twirled to the strains of a Strauss waltz.

Her partner, a tall, distinguished-looking Frenchman, smiled down at her. '*Mademoiselle, je suis enchanté!* Do not, I pray, worry that we are the only ones who dance. They are eating their hearts out with jealousy at my luck in dancing with you.'

Alexia laughed up at him. 'Flattery will get you everywhere, *monsieur!*'

'Really?' his arms tightened about her.

'No,' she laughed again, 'not really!' and concentrated on the steps of the dance, not having waltzed since her days at school.

The music stopped and there was a round of applause for the two dancers. The Frenchman escorted her back to the table, where Rafael was sitting with his arm around one of the lovely blonde girls he had brought with him. He nodded coldly to Alexia as he rose to lead the girl on to the dance floor.

To hell with him! she thought angrily, feeling almost faint with jealousy as he clasped the blonde tightly in his arms.

The Frenchman, Pierre something-or-other, was clearly, as he said, enchanted with her, and she found his admiration a soothing balm for her unhappy spirits. She allowed him to monopolise her as he claimed dance after dance. Anything was better than having to sit by and watch Rafael being mobbed by women.

Word had soon got around that he was present, and if she hadn't been so cross at the way he was studiously ignoring her, she would have felt sorry for him. No wonder he hadn't wanted to come, she thought, remembering his reluctance to comply with Julia's wish at lunch all those days ago. She watched as he tried to extricate himself, with some difficulty from the embrace of a fat, overdressed lady of uncertain years, only to fall victim, moments later, to the clutches of a group of blue-rinsed matrons from the mid-west of America.

Serve him right, she thought as she swept past him, head held high, on her way to the supper table. She was escorted by Alfonso and also Pierre, who had refused to leave her side. 'It is pistols at dawn!' he hissed laughingly at Alfonso, who in reply, twirled an imaginary moustache as he answered, 'How like you French frogs—no panache! Here in Spain, we prefer the sword.'

'O.K., *mon brave*,' said Pierre, 'that suits me. You wave your sword and I will shoot you dead!' Their joint roar of laughter practically filled the small supper room.

'Come on, you two,' Alexia called. 'I'm hungry! You can sort it out later.'

'Such a cold-hearted woman!' moaned Pierre, as plates in hand they helped themselves from the delicious buffet table.

Much later, she was walking on the terrace outside as Pierre flirted outrageously with her, when Rafael approached and asked for a dance.

'Go away,' Pierre demanded. 'I am busy persuading this lovely girl that she is about to become as madly in love with me as I am with her. Go away at once!'

'I doubt that you will succeed,' Rafael said grimly.

'You never know,' said Alexia blandly, her heart beginning to pound. 'Pierre is being very persuasive!' She smiled brilliantly at the Frenchman, feeling sick with apprehension and wondering how to get out of dancing with Rafael.

Unfortunately Pierre yielded with good grace. 'Go now, and come back soon, *chérie*.'

She rose reluctantly, allowing Rafael to lead her on to the dance floor. The band were playing softly, the lights dimmer than they had been earlier in the evening.

'You appear to have made a conquest,' he said grimly, taking her into his arms.

'He's very amusing and he makes me laugh,' Alexia answered lightly. Here we go again, she thought unhappily, her stomach knotting with tension as he drew her closer to him. 'You also,' she added, 'appear to have made quite a few conquests tonight.'

'Yes, I do, don't I?' he agreed sardonically as she flushed at having displayed her jealousy so clearly. 'However,' he continued, 'none so distinguished as yours.'

'Pierre? He's sweet!'

'I don't think the Comte de Guigne is used to being referred to as "sweet",' he said dryly.

'What a snob you are, Rafael!' she countered swifly. 'I didn't know he had a title, and—and it wouldn't have made any difference if I had. He's charming,' she added, in an enthusiastic voice which she hoped would annoy him. 'Really very charming. I like him enormously.'

'Cool it, Alexia,' he replied. 'Why don't we stop knifing each other and just dance . . . hm?'

She hid her burning face in his shoulder as they swayed gently to the music. Placing a warm hand underneath her long hair, he gently stroked the back of her neck. Ripples of excitement danced across her skin at his touch and she did not pull away as he clasped her even tighter to his hard, firm body.

They completed the dance in silence and in silence Rafael returned her to Pierre with an ironic bow, before going over to a hot-eyed brunette with a truly amazing bust, who greeted him with an enthusiastic kiss.

The swine, Alexia thought miserably, while she chatted brightly to Pierre. He knows he can cut me out of the herd and brand me, any time he likes!

She was silent during the journey home, but it didn't matter as Julia prattled vivaciously in Spanish to Doña Maria, while Rafael, who was driving, was practically monosyllabic.

'It's been a super evening,' Julia said to her brother as they arrived back at the house. 'Thank you so much for letting me go. Do you know,' she said to Alexia, 'I think I've got in a muddle. I seem to have two boys taking me out tomorrow night—isn't it wonderful!'

'Wonderful,' Alexia smiled faintly as she got out of the car.

She was saying goodnight and thanking Doña Maria for the dress once again, when Rafael came in from putting the vehicle away in the garage.

'Alexia,' he said, 'may I please have a word with you? I won't keep you long.'

She hesitated, but there was little she could say in front of his mother and Julia. Shrugging, she allowed him to issue her into the study.

'Will you have a drink?' he asked, as he poured himself a whisky.

'No, thank you.' She remained standing silently as he walked to the desk and sat down.

'Well,' he told her, swinging around in the chair, his long, elegant legs stretched out before him, a piece of paper in his hand, 'I had a very interesting telephone call from my solicitor in London this evening. Very interesting. Won't you sit down?'

'No, thank you,' she said tonelessly, beginning to feel sick.

'Very well. There is no doubt that you have puzzled me, Alexia. Your accusations, about my obsessive interest in your background, are entirely right. Following our little lunch party, when Michael told me what a clever girl you were, the two and two I had been trying to add up simply didn't make sense.' He leaned back in the chair and regarded her with hard eyes. 'So I set some enquiries in train. Really very stupid of me not to do it before, wasn't it? And my goodness, what a can of worms it all turned out to be!' His scathing voice pierced her like a knife and she sank down, trembling, on to a low stool. 'In point of fact, it has a neat chronological order, doesn't it? Let me see . . .' He studied the paper in front of him.

'First we have the birth certificate of Antonia Harrison, followed two years later by that of her sister

Alexia—who, it appears, is going to be twenty-four next November. There follows a long pause in the story and then we have the birth of little Juan Valverde. The certificate is quite explicit: father Luis Valverde ... quite right and proper. But surprise, surprise! His mother is not the good Alexia, as we had all supposed. No indeed! It is her sister, Antonia Harrison, who, alas, is not married to the said Luis. Any comments, Alexia?'

'No,' she whispered.

'The accused reserves her defence? Quite right! Where was I? Oh yes. The next certificate is not a happy one. Poor Antonia dies, aged twenty-one, only a few days after her son's birth. My solicitor, by the way, tells me that you filled out the forms and informed the authorities. Or so the document states?'

'Yes,' she cleared her throat. 'Yes, I—I did.'

'Now we come to the apogee of this little drama. We find that only one month after his ... er ... girl-friend's death, Luis Valverde, aged twenty-two, marries Alexia Harrison, aged nineteen, a spinster of the parish, who gives her occupation as a student. My word,' his voice dripped with sarcasm, 'you're a quick worker, I'll say that for you!'

Alexia sat silent, staring blindly at Rafael.

'You've also got to hand it to my brother,' he laughed harshly. 'Off with the old and on with the new ... He really must have been a lot more attractive than I ever supposed! *Por Dios*, Alexia, you really fooled me, didn't you?' His dark eyes flashed angrily at the girl as she sat in a pool of rumpled lace, her green eyes gazing fixedly back at him.

There was a long, long pause, as their eyes remained locked together. Eventually Alexia gave a deep sigh and said sadly, 'No one fooled you, Rafael ... no one.

You—you only fooled yourself, and it—it would seem that you're continuing to do so.'

She rose, slowly walking over to stand by the door before turning to face him.

'You'd made up your mind as to the facts of the case before you met me . . . and you're still drawing the wrong conclusions. I'm not going to argue or—or defend myself and my sister,' she said with quiet dignity. 'I've told your mother the truth, so I suggest that you talk to her. I—I'm going to bed. Goodnight.'

'Oh no, you don't!' Rafael leapt from his chair, striding quickly over to grab her arm. 'I want the truth . . . and I want it now!'

'No. I have said all I'm going to say on the subject. As for the "truth" . . . what is that? I've told your mother the truth as I see it. Whether you believe it is another matter.'

She sighed deeply, as he stared silently into her eyes. 'Rafael, it—it's late and I'm tired. It's been a long day and I didn't sleep very well last night. Can't you—can't you understand that I don't want any more fights. I really don't. I—I hate all our arguments, they make me so unhappy.' Alexia swayed wearily.

He gently drew her towards him, where she leant unresisting against his shoulder.

'*Querida*,' he whispered into her hair, 'I too have no wish to fight or argue. I—I do not know what comes over me sometimes.' He lifted her face slowly to his, looking deep into her eyes. 'You—you have bewitched me . . . I . . . Oh God!' he groaned, his mouth seeking the softly scented warmth of her bare shoulders, before claiming the parted sweetness of his lips. Loving him as she did, she couldn't resist as his mouth moved over hers in a kiss of burning possession. As always, he ignited a flame within her as hungrily she moved her slim figure sensually against him.

'*Dios!* What a passionate woman you are,' he murmured huskily, trailing his lips over her face. 'It is late, but I–I cannot bear to let you go. Holy Mother of God, how you tempt me!'

Alexia gazed up at Rafael, his face a taut mask of unconcealed desire, feeling her knees buckle as an answering shaft of passionate need coursed through her veins. She whimpered with fright at the intensity of her emotion, as he held her tightly against him for a moment, before he opened the door and pushed her into the hall.

'Upstairs!' he commanded, in a voice that shook with suppressed tension. 'Upstairs quickly, or we will both by very sorry.'

She stood looking at him helplessly, then turned and slowly climbed the stairs to her room.

CHAPTER NINE

ALEXIA woke early as the morning sun began to creep into her room. Lying back on the soft pillows, she stared blindly at the ceiling trying hard to contemplate with equanimity the remaining two weeks of her holiday in Spain. She had known that Rafael would be angry when he found out that Juan was not her son, but she could never have imagined just how cruel he would be. Although it had ended so passionately, the scene downstairs last night had been a searing experience.

She felt a pang of guilt as she acknowledged that she was not blameless in the matter. She hadn't deliberately set out to fool him, but when Rafael had made the original mistake, she had let him believe it.

Rafael ... the muscles in her stomach contracted and her body throbbed as she remembered his burning kisses, the firm, hard strength of his arms ... Suddenly, something he had said last night filled her mind to the exclusion of all else. 'You have bewitched me!' Surely ...? Yes, of course! His song at Jerry's party. He—he wrote that song for me, she thought. He really did write it *for me!*

She knew it was ridiculous, but—but if he cared enough to write a song about his feelings for her, then maybe ... She sat up in bed hugging her knees, as her mind trailed off on a happy daydream. It was rudely interrupted some time later by Juan. With tousled hair, and clutching his pyjama bottoms, he climbed into bed with her, demanding his breakfast.

'Honestly!' Alexia laughed. 'I don't know how you stay so thin, you never stop eating! All right, let's get you dressed and then we'll find Rosa. I expect you'll be able to persuade her to give you an early breakfast in the kitchen.'

'Oh good!' He jumped up and down on the bed.

'You're becoming a spoilt brat!' she smilingly accused him.

'I know. It's super here in Spain,' he giggled.

'Come on, you horrid little boy. You'll soon be as bad as your Uncle Rafael!'

'But I like Uncle Rafael. He's a nice man and he spoils me too!'

Rosa had, of course, welcomed Juan with open arms. Shooing Alexia back to bed, she promised to bring up a breakfast tray later. Apparently Doña Maria had decided that everyone should have a lie-in to recover from the ball the night before.

An hour later Alexia put down her empty coffee cup and went over to the small desk by the window, to catch up with her correspondence. She really ought to write to Melanie as she had promised she would. It would be difficult, though, not to let her eagle-eyed friend gain some insight into her problems. Maybe she could concentrate on describing the ball last night? Melanie would be thrilled to hear about Pierre, for instance.

She was well into her letter, describing the nightclub and the wonderful dresses worn by the women, when the sound of raised voices began to distract her. By the time she was fully aware of what appeared to be a tremendous row, there was only one voice to be heard, as a torrent of Spanish flowed through the house. It—it was Doña Maria, she realised with amazement.

The voice ceased on a high note, followed by the slamming of a door. A long pause was punctuated by the front door being banged with such force that it shook the whole house, succeeded by the sound of a car roaring off into the distance.

It's—it's like some radio play, she thought, bewildered. Crash, bang, smash, wallop! How extraordinary.

Half an hour later, there was a knock on the door and Rosa appeared with the most enormous bunch of white roses that Alexia had ever seen. 'For you,' Rosa gasped, tears running down her cheeks.

'Rosa!' Alexia jumped up. 'What's the matter?' Concerned, she ran to the old woman, taking the flowers and tossing them over on to the bed, before leading her to an easy chair. 'Are you all right?' she asked anxiously.

Rosa gasped as she rocked to and fro, it taking Alexia some moments to realise that the old nanny wasn't crying. She was laughing! Laughing so much that she had trouble catching her breath.

She waited while Rosa calmed down. 'What's all this about? What was all that noise, for heaven's sake?'

Wiping the tears from her eyes, Rosa tried to compose herself, but deep chuckles kept on shaking her fat old figure.

'Don Rafael . . .' she started laughing again. 'Oh, *señora!* Don Rafael . . . he go "poof" . . . He explode!'

'But why? Oh, do stop laughing, Rosa! Come on, tell me what's happening?'

'His *mamá*, she is very angry with him. *Muy, muy.* I listen at door.'

'Oh, Rosa!'

'Why not?' she shrugged. 'Is my family, no? Doña Maria, she tells him he very bad, very naughty. He is not kind to you. Poor Doña Alexia, she say, then she tell him all. How you so kind and work so hard for Luis and Juan.'

'Oh lord! It's all my fault.' Alexia sank down onto a chair, feeling sick and miserable.

'No! Doña Maria say you good girl, *señora*. Poor Don Rafael, he kept saying, "*No sabia. No sabia*"—"I didn't know"—and Doña Maria say he stupid. *Ola!* She told him!' Rosa started to laugh again.

'But that's not funny at all.' Alexia gazed at Rosa in distress. 'It's awful that Rafael and his mother should quarrel . . . really bad,' she explained earnestly.

'No, no! Is good for Don Rafael. He has been a naughty boy . . . yes? He came out of his *mamá*'s room with such a face . . . oh, very cross, and he see me with the roses for you. He look at the card . . .' Rosa started laughing again, '. . . and he jump up and down with rage. Very funny!'

'Who in the world would send me such a bunch of roses?' Alexia went over to the bed, and extracted the card. 'Oh . . .' The card read: 'For a wonderful woman. A wonderful night to remember . . . may there be many more of them! Pierre, Comte de Guigne.'

'Don Rafael,' he swear and he curse. Oh, he is so jealous, is good, no?'

Alexia couldn't stop herself from grinning sheepishly. 'Yes Rosa, it's . . . er . . . very good.' She blushed, then remembered the noise of the argument. 'Poor Doña Maria, she must be so upset.'

'Why you think I laugh? We have been laughing together. His *mamá*, she say, serve him right. Teach him a lesson. Is good for him. We laugh, and then we cry for poor Luis, and then we laugh again. Is life, no?'

'Rosa,' Alexia gestured hopelessly, 'I—I don't want him to be upset . . .'

'Yes—yes, you do. Don Rafael is my baby. I tell you, is good for him. His *mamá* agree. He is mad for you, because he love you. I, Rosa, I know him. He love you, *mucho, mucho*. He . . .' she made a gesture to her eyes, 'he . . . squint . . . yes?'

'Squint? Can't see?' Alexia struggled to interpret Rosa's words. 'See crooked? Can't see straight?'

'*Sí, sí.* He is so angry, so jealous, he cannot see straight. He is very . . . er . . .' Rosa made a grabbing motion, 'mine, mine . . .'

'Possessive?'

'Is right. Possessive. "All mine", he is saying. But Luis—Luis is dead. He cannot fight dead man, no?'

'But Rosa, Luis was never really a—a proper husband . . .'

'Doña Maria she tell me so. But Don Rafael, he not know that. His *mamá* say you do not want him to know. He love you, and he wish to be your first man. Not follow his brother, *comprende?*' Rosa got up to leave.

'No,' said Alexia, shaking her head. 'No, you're wrong. He doesn't love me.' He just wants me sexually, she thought sadly.

'We will see,' laughed Rosa, as she waddled from the room.

Alexia felt too overwhelmed by the events of the morning to cope with any of the Valverde family, Rafael or otherwise. Taking the small car which she had been urged to use, she and Juan went off to a beach outside Marbella where they spent the day. Dusk was falling by the time they returned, tired and full of sun and sea air.

'Come on, Juan, it's past your bedtime.' Alexia carried the sleepy little boy upstairs. 'I'll just give you a bath to get rid of the sand, and then . . . Oh, my goodness!'

She stood transfixed at the entrance to her bedroom.
The whole room was full of red roses. Vases and vases
of red roses! The effect was amazing and she sat
weakly down on her bed, completely bemused.

'Rosa,' she cried, as the old woman came smiling
into her room, 'that Frenchman has gone mad!'

'Is no Frenchman! Here, this is for you.' Rosa gave
Alexia an envelope. 'Don Rafael said for you to please
read, not to destroy.' She looked around the room.
'Red roses for passion ... *Muy Español* ... *muy, muy
Español!* I tell you, you see, Rosa is right!' She
laughed and took Juan off to his bath.

Alexia sat still, stunned by the sight of so many
roses filling the room with their scent. Passion?—yes.
But love?—no. She put the envelope down unopened
on her bedside table before going to stare blindly out
of her window. Rosa returned with Juan, freshly
bathed and powdered, and Alexia tucked him up in
bed, kissing him good night.

'I would like supper in my room tonight, please,
Rosa,' she said, suddenly feeling exhausted.

'*Si*. You will read letter? I promise Don Rafael.'

'Yes,' she sighed, 'I'll read it ... later.'

Clearly disappointed at not being told the letter's
contents, Rosa left the room.

Rosa's a dear, thought Alexia, as she lay in the
bath, but she still thinks Rafael's a little boy. She
simply wouldn't understand his wanting to have an
affair with any presentable woman he met. That sort
of life is outside her understanding. Love indeed!
That's a laugh, she told herself bitterly.

Bathed and dressed in a caftan, she moved
distracted around the room, glancing at the letter from
time to time. Suddenly full of resolution, she walked
over and slit the envelope. It contained one piece of

paper, covered in Rafael's fine italic writing. Moving slowly over to a chair, she sat down to read the short missive.

> *'Alexia, I have been a crass fool and am covered in mortification. Realising that it is too much to hope for, I nevertheless do beg you to forgive one who is now in an agony of remorse. Rafael.'*

Rosa, arriving with the supper tray, found Alexia lying on the bed weeping for her hopeless love. For once the old nanny said nothing, but merely sat down and gathered the slim, unhappy girl to her large bosom. Murmuring soft, soothing sounds, she rocked her back and fro as she would comfort a child.

Going heavy-eyed down to breakfast the next morning, Alexia was halted by a call from Doña Maria's room. Sending Juan on down to his meal, she went slowly along the corridor and entered the prettily furnished sitting room.

'Ah, my dear,' Doña Maria smiled from a chair, 'do come in. Did you sleep well?'

'Yes, thank you.' She had in fact slept like a log, totally exhausted by all that had happened and by her emotional storm of tears. Weeping for what could never be.

'My son has asked me to be present. I hope that you do not mind?'

Alexia spun around, startled to see Rafael standing behind her.

'Oh no, I . . .' She turned away in confusion.

'Alexia,' Rafael's voice was low and husky, 'I did want my mother to be here to witness my deep apology to you. She is absolutely right, there is no way I, or my family, can repay the debt that we owe you. It's—it's beyond my power. I—I ...' he floundered helplessly as he gazed at her averted figure.

Alexia turned slowly to face him. 'Rafael, of course I—I forgive you. There's little to forgive. I told your mother that I was partly to blame. I ... er ... I was frightened of losing Juan, and ... well, my personal feelings of—of anger against you also got in the way of the truth.' She sighed as she looked at his strained face and stiff, rigid figure. My poor Rafael, she thought, filled with aching compassion for the man she loved. How making this apology must wound him, he was such a proud man.

'What is past is past,' she continued. 'Luis and my sister are dead. Our duty, surely, is to the living, as—as aunt and uncle to Juan. I've already told your mother that I'll be happy for him to come here, to Spain, as often as you both wish. You were right, in London. Juan should get to know his native country.'

'Alexia, I ...'

'Please, Rafael, let's forget the whole miserable upset and be friends. I don't think I can stand any more arguments.' Alexia brushed a weary hand through her hair. 'All these ... these rows, they're just too much for me to cope with.'

Rafael moved slowly forward, clasping her trembling fingers and gazing down into her face. Slowly he raised her hands to his lips, kissing each in turn. 'It shall be as you say, Alexia. I give you my word,' he said quietly. 'There will be no more rows—no more arguments. You are indeed a generous woman.'

Alexia blushed under his dark gaze as Doña Maria gave a dry cough. 'I think,' his mother said firmly, 'that it is now time for breakfast.'

Rafael was little in evidence the next few days as he

rehearsed for his forthcoming charity concert to be
held in the bullring at Ronda. Apart from his jogging
figure on the beach in the mornings, Alexia did not set
eyes on him for three days. Three days of peace and
quiet, which did much to soothe her battered emotions
as she struggled to accept the hopelessness of her love
for Rafael.

She was sitting by the pool one morning, chatting
idly to Doña Maria, when Rafael suddenly appeared
carrying a folder which seemed to contain sheets of
music.

'I'm just off to Ronda to check that everything is
ready for the concert,' he said, 'but I'd love some
coffee before I go, Mamá.'

'Of course. Alexia, would you please be so good as
to fetch another cup?'

Alexia hurried off to the kitchen, grateful for the
opportunity to cool her flushed cheeks in private. All
her good resolutions, all her reasoned arguments had
vanished at the sight of Rafael's tall, handsome figure.
She closed her eyes, leaning weakly against the china
cupboard as she was swept by a dizzy, trembling
longing for his warm embrace. She splashed her
burning face with cold water before returning to find
mother and son chatting together in Spanish, which
ceased with her arrival.

'It occurs to me,' said Doña Maria as she poured the
coffee, 'that if you are going to Ronda, Rafael, you might
take Alexia with you.' She turned to the girl. 'We have a
house there—well, it's Rafael's really. My father left it
and the land to him, when he died. It lies empty for most
of the year and I would be so grateful if you could check
that it hasn't been broken into and vandalised.'

'But—but surely Rafael can see to it?' Alexia looked
at her in bewilderment.

'No, dear,' Doña Maria replied firmly. 'That sort of inspection requires the feminine touch, as I'm sure you will agree. It would please me if you agreed to go, it would mean that I did not have to worry about the house—you understand?

Alexia glanced swiftly at Rafael, who was apparently not listening to the exchange between his mother and Alexia, but seemed absorbed by the musical score in front of him.

'Well,' she shrugged, 'I—I really don't see what I can do, but—but if you really think . . .'

'Thank you so much, my dear. It will be a great help. There is no need to worry about Juan. I'll look after him.'

Alexia still felt puzzled. There were overtones to this request that she was unable to pin down. Mother and son seemed to be acting normally, but . . . 'When do you want to go?' she asked Rafael.

He looked up, the heavy eyelids masking all expression in his dark eyes. 'As soon as possible. It's a longish drive.'

The white Mercedes sports car snaked its way around the mountainsides of the Serrania de Ronda. From San Pedro de Alcantara on the coast, the route was uphill all the way. The road had been carved from the sides of the mountains, and was so narrow in places that passing another vehicle was a hazardous occupation.

Alexia glanced sideways at Rafael's stern profile as he concentrated on his driving. He had been strangely silent and withdrawn since acceding to his mother's wish that Alexia should accompany him to Ronda. Not unfriendly, but somehow distant. Her gaze trailed to his shirt sleeves, rolled up to display his deeply tanned

muscular arms, and his long slim hands, busily
turning the wheel this way and that. As he operated
the short gear stick, his hand occasionally brushed her
leg, but if he noticed the contact, he gave no sign.

As the journey progressed, she began to relax in the
warmth of the sunny day, revelling in the breeze
which lifted and caught her hair, tied in a bow behind
her neck. Rafael pointed out places of interest, his
bland, matter-of-fact tone of voice having a palliative
and calming effect on her initial breathless nervousness
at their close proximity.

'Tell me about Ronda. Is it a very old town?' she asked.

'Very old. There was a settlement there in Roman
times, I believe, a little south of the present town. We
Spaniards,' Rafael said proudly, 'contributed much to
the Roman Empire. The Emperor Trajan and Seneca
the poet, for instance, were Spanish. Spain was part of
the Roman Empire,' he explained, 'and Julius Caesar
and his rival Pompey fought a great battle near
Ronda.'

Rafael paused as he negotiated a tricky bend. 'This
area of Spain was ruled by the Turkish Ottoman
Empire after the Romans, while Ronda itself was a
Muslim city for hundreds of years. Eventually, the
Christians rose against the Muslims and finally drove
them from the country.' He grinned at Alexia. 'You
see, I remember my history lessons from school.'

'Excellent! You're doing very well. Go on.'

'Well, as for Ronda, there was a great battle and it
was captured by King Ferdinand in May 1485. The
date is remembered in my family, because an ancestor
of my grandfather fought beside the King in that
battle. After the victory, along with other knights he
was granted property and land as a reward for his
services. We still own a house and much of the land.'

'That's about five hundred years ago,' Alexia calculated. 'I'm surprised that the family and their possessions should have survived so long.'

'Ah,' he laughed, glancing sideways, 'did you not know? We are a very tenacious lot, Alexia!' She flushed at the mocking gleam in his eyes as he continued. 'Of course, land has come and gone. It is not always easy in times of war and famine, the last Civil War in Spain, in the 1930s, was an especially bad time. However, the house my mother wishes you to look at is part of the original gift. It was the old palace of the Muslim ruler of Ronda, Abd el-Malik. In gratitude, my ancestor named it Castillo del Rey— Castle of the King.'

Rafael slowed down suddenly and turning the wheel, pulled across the road to a large parking area.

'Come, I want to show you something,' he said, opening the car door and walking to the edge of the cliff. He leaned on the railings looking out over the valley gorge far beyond them, turning to smile at Alexia as she joined him. 'I always stop here, it's so beautiful,' he said simply, turning back to admire the view.

'It's breathtaking!' She was stunned by the rugged beauty of the tree-covered mountainsides. From a cleft in a rock nearby, a stream gushed forth, sending a spray of myriad glistening drops falling, almost in slow motion, to the valley far below.

'Oh, look! she called, pointing to the sky. 'Aren't they wonderful! What kind of bird are they?'

'Ah, I was hoping we'd see some. They're eagles. Yes, they are a wonderful sight.'

Alexia watched entranced as the great birds swept down the mountainsides, only to wheel and soar upwards on the currents of rising air.

He spoke quietly. 'I was very close to my grandfather and used to spend the summer holidays here in Ronda with him. We would often come to watch the eagles fly so fast and free.'

Rafael remained lost in his thoughts for some time. 'It was a bad summer for me, after my father died. I had to decide what to do—to continue with my studies, or to try and make money for my *familia*.' His unconscious use of the Spanish word betrayed his emotional absorption in his past.

'My grandfather brought me here and pointed out how the birds soared above the rocks. He showed me that there was no shame in becoming a man who sang rather silly songs, but that I should rise like the eagles, to meet the challenges of life. One can be free in one's heart, after all.'

Alexia stood very still, hardly daring to breathe. This was a side of Rafael that she had never seen, and she was unaccountably touched that he should have revealed it to her.

They continued to stand in silence for a long time, before he sighed and taking her hand led her back to the car.

'The eagles, they are so beautiful. Thank you for showing them to me,' she said quietly, as he started the car.

'They are always there, for those who have eyes to see.' He smiled enigmatically at her as they resumed their journey.

They were approaching the town when she asked the question that had been puzzling her. 'Why a bullring? I mean, surely that's where they have bullfights, isn't it? Why do you hold your concert in a bullring of all places?'

'It's fairly simple,' he answered. 'First of all, I need

space. Although I know you will accuse me of being swollen-headed and arrogant, Alexia,' he smiled briefly at her, 'I'm afraid a lot of people will come to hear me sing. I always take a month off in the summer, but I have for some years given a charity concert in Ronda. Frankly, there isn't anywhere else that is suitable.

'I will have nothing to do with the sort of open-air concert that is held in fields and contains more drug-pushers than people wishing to hear the music. So the bullring in Ronda is perfect.' He slowed down as they began to wind their way through the narrow streets. 'It is also,' he said, 'the oldest such ring in Spain. Very beautiful, as you will see.'

He stopped the car. 'Now, I am going to give you a fright,' and helping her out, he led her back to the stone bridge over which they had just driven, and on to a parapet. 'Look down,' he commanded, laughing as she staggered back, clutching his arm in panic. Spread below her was an almost paralysing view of a deep chasm with a torrent of water flowing through the base, which lay about five hundred feet below.

'I've never ... I've never seen anything like it before,' she muttered, feeling dizzy and slightly sick. 'I know you're proud of Ronda, Rafael, but could we move back a bit? It's all—all rather terrifying. I don't think I've got much of a head for heights.'

'You can see now why it was a long hard battle for my ancestor and the King. This town was practically impossible to conquer.' He took her arm. 'Come on, we'll have some lunch before I have to start work.'

Sitting on the terrace of the Hotel Victoria after lunch, Alexia was filled with wonder as she gazed across the peaks of the Serrania spread out before the terraced gardens of the hotel. The colours of the far mountains ranged from pale elephant grey to soft blues, magentas and lilacs.

'It's a magnificent sight. I'm not surprised that you love it here.' She turned to smile at Rafael, her cheeks flushing as she realised he had been looking at her and not at the wonderful view.

'Alas,' he sighed, 'I must go and do some work. I suggest that I leave you here, to finish your coffee. When you feel like it, you can come along to the bullring—it's not far and very easy to find. Please take your time and explore the town if you wish. I will be occupied for at least two hours, possibly more.'

'That sounds lovely, Rafael. But what about the house? Your mother seemed very concerned about it.'

'We will go there later. I must work now,' he said firmly, in a tone that brooked no argument. '*Adios*, I will see you later.'

She watched his tall figure as he strode back across the terrace, where he was met by a waiter who bowed obsequiously. It proved a sharp contrast in style; the waiter in his uniform and Rafael in a pair of faded, hip-hugging jeans and a pale blue casual shirt with rolled up sleeves.

Alexia had protested that she wasn't dressed properly, as they arrived at the large hotel. Rafael had looked down at her, not having been given time to change before the journey, she was wearing the cream silk blouse and matching slim cotton trousers in which she had dressed that morning. She had blushed under his gaze, the gleam in his hooded eyes revealing that he was fully aware she wore nothing beneath her blouse.

'You look fine to me,' he said blandly, although he had insisted that she wore her hair loose. 'If I'm paying for your lunch, the least you can do is to wear your hair the way I like it,' he had added firmly, reaching over to untie the ribbon. She had shivered at the touch of his warm fingers as they had brushed the back of her neck, but he gave no sign of noticing her reaction to his touch.

It was during lunch that she was again reminded of his 'star' status. He had been quickly recognised by the other people in the hotel restaurant, an excited murmur running around the room. Living in his house and seeing him every day she was apt, not surprisingly, to forget his profession.

The bullring was obviously very old. Alexia stood outside, looking at its round white walls and tiled roof, before going in through a large Baroque door. Passing through to the ring inside, she sat down on a bench to take in her surroundings.

The inside of the ring had stone barriers, which seemed unusual—surely they were normally made of wood? She looked up at the two arcaded storeys, held up by old stone columns. Across the open sandy space of the ring itself she saw Rafael talking earnestly to Alfonso and another man, while carpenters were putting the final touches to a large rectangular stage in the middle of the arena. Various musicians were checking their drums, guitars, keyboards and amplifiers, the air filled with odd, discordant noises.

On the way, she had walked through some public gardens full of roses, petunias and trees in full, fragile blossom. Sitting on a bench, shaded by a whispering acacia tree which threw a light blue, dappled shade over her, she had looked across to the range of mountains opposite, drinking in the view.

Sitting now in the bullring, she thought that of the little she'd seen of Spain. Ronda must be one of the loveliest places. She could understand Rafael's fondness for his ancestral roots.

The musicians had begun to play a tune with a steady disco beat. She thought it sounded fine, but Rafael immediately turned and ran leaping on to the stage, indicating that he wanted a slightly slower tempo. She couldn't see his face clearly as the sun was in her eyes, but she was impressed with his hard work as the afternoon wore on. He only sang a few bars, being mostly concerned with carefully checking each instrument and the microphones.

She heard a step and turned to see Alfonso coming to sit down beside her, mopping his brow.

'*Por dios*, the sun is hot today! Rafael works hard—no?'

'He seems to be taking a great deal of trouble. I didn't know putting on a concert like this involved so much work.'

'*Si, si*, he is a complete professional. Great attention to detail is the difference between success and failure. You have read stories of pop stars with drugs, drink and women?'

'Yes, I—I suppose so.'

Alfonso laughed. 'They do not survive. To be a success in this business, you must live like a monk—really. Keep fit, sleep well and work, work, work!'

Alexia looked throughtfully at him as she considered his words.

'You think: Hah, old Alfonso is giving me a message. *Si?* You are right. Do not believe what you read, my dear Alexia. I tell you, Rafael does not take drugs, he drinks very little, and although the women offer, he does not accept!' He laughed again. 'Oh yes, he likes women very much. But not casually, you understand. Of course, when he was young . . .' he shrugged. 'Well, we all do things when we are young that we prefer to forget. But I know him. I know him very well—like a father. So I know it is important I tell you this. No?'

Alexia blushed, turning away in confusion from Alfonso's wise eyes to stare blindly at the musicians putting the covers over their instruments.

'Ah well,' he sighed dramatically, 'if I were twenty years younger, I would cut him out. As it is, I'm just a poor old man . . .'

She laughed and kissed him on the cheek. 'I think you're a lovely "old man", Alfonso!'

'*Dios!* I leave her for just a short time,' a voice came from behind them, 'and when I return, I find her kissing a man—it's disgraceful!' Alexia turned quickly to see Rafael, his dark handsome face creased by a wide grin. 'We cannot take her anywhere. It is very sad,' he explained in a weary voice to Alfonso. 'The doctor suggests tranquillisers in the Naafi tea, but we don't hold out much hope . . .'

'What is this "Naffi tea"?' queried Alfonso, clearly mystified. He could obtain no answer from Rafael, who was doubled up with laughter, or from Alexia, whose lovely face was covered by a tide of deep crimson.

'You're very unkind to remind me of that. It's—it's not fair,' she protested, her face still pink with embarrassment as he led her towards the car.

'Quite right—it isn't. Come, we will go to the house now.' Rafael drove slowly through the ancient town. Alexia, thankful for the breeze which cooled her fevered cheeks, noticed large posters advertising his concert tomorrow.

'Do you mind? Seeing your face on the posters, I mean?' she asked.

'No, I've got so used to it.' He shrugged. 'It was very strange at first, but now I hardly notice. Here we are,' he added, as they arrived at a large ancient stone house.

The huge brass-studded oak door opened at their approach and they were welcomed inside by a fat, elderly woman, dressed in black, who greeted Rafael with enthusiasm.

'Ha! Don Rafael!' she cried, kissing him on both cheeks and proceeding to rattle off a stream of Spanish, to which he replied in the same language.

'*Gracias—gracias*, Teresa. *Hasta mañana*,' he said, as the woman smiled and left them standing amidst vaulting Moorish arches in a large hall.

'We will now inspect the house,' he said, leading her through the many rooms, all of which, Alexia noticed, were in perfect condition. The floors shone, the furniture gleamed with polish and even the windows looked as if they had been cleaned that day.

The rooms seemed to be built around three courtyards, each containing a small fountain and shady trees. Eventually, as dusk was falling, they came to a tree-lined terraced garden which, like the hotel, looked across the Sierra.

'Sit down, Alexia,' said Rafael, indicating a stone bench covered with striped cushions, 'and I will get us a drink.'

She did as he suggested, looking out at the mountains, her mind in turmoil. 'It's getting dark,' she said quietly as he returned with a bottle of chilled white wine.

'Yes, it is.' His voice was noncommittal.

'I—I don't think your house needed an inspection by me,' she stated in the same quiet tone.

'No, it didn't,' he agreed, busily engaged in

drawing the cork and pouring the wine. There was a pause as he handed her a glass, before coming to sit down on the bench beside her. 'As you say, it is late. I think we may as well spend the night here . . . don't you?' Rafael's voice was devoid of any expression as he looked straight ahead at the mountains.

Alexia opened her mouth to protest, then closed it again slowly. She had been right, by the pool this morning. Mother and son had arranged this trip. His mother had not only approved but . . . Rafael's voice interrupting her thoughts, confirmed her suspicions.

'Do not worry about Juan, my mother is not expecting us back tonight.'

She glanced at him. His hooded eyes were clear and held no message for her as he looked blandly back at her in the gathering dusk.

She turned away, gazing sightlessly at the view before her. She ought to say something . . . she really ought. The silence lengthened between them as they sipped their wine. Alexia's bemused mind tried to overcome the extraordinary feeling of helpless languor and inertia which seemed to have her firmly in its grip.

'This house means a great deal to me,' Rafael said quietly. 'I am committed to one more world series of concerts, finishing up in South America; then I plan to retire.' He laughed softly in the darkness. 'I don't want to become that sad creature, an ageing pop star! So I'm intending to live here and farm the land my grandfather left me. Can you see me as a farmer, Alexia?'

'Well I . . .'

'Yes, perhaps it sounds incongruous. However, I intend to try. Of course, I'm lucky in that I have accumulated enough money, certainly enough not to have to work if I don't want to. But that is no life for a

man. No, I shall work the land. I am looking forward
to it.'

'I . . . er . . . I think you'll succeed at whatever you
chose to do,' she said reflectively.

'Alexia! Such a compliment from you. I am
overwhelmed! Are you sure you are feeling well?' She
could feel his shoulders shaking beside her, unable to
suppress his amusement.

'Oh . . . pooh!' she said vulgarly, the quiver in her
voice betraying her rueful grin.

'Ah, that's more like the Alexia I know and love!
Would you like some more wine, or shall we go and
explore the kitchen? I don't know whether Teresa has
left us anything to eat, so you may have to provide a
miracle with a loaf and no fishes.'

Alexia took a deep breath. This was . . . this was
positively the last opportunity she had to demand to
be taken back home to Juan. It was clearly what she
ought to do . . . 'The Alexia I know and love' . . .? But
he didn't love her . . . did he? Her wildly beating heart
fought a swift internal battle against cautious sense as
the thoughts and counter-thoughts struggled back and
forth through her confused mind.

'Well, Alexia?' Rafael's voice cut into the silence.

With some astonishment she heard herself say, 'I
. . . er . . . I think I'd like some more wine, and . . .
and then . . . er . . . then you can lead me to the
kitchen.'

Rafael finished the last of his cheese omelette and sat
back sighing. 'Anyone who can whip up such a dish
for the gods is undoubtedly—as the Good Book
says—a pearl beyond price!'

Alexia smiled softly. 'Don't tell me I've found your
Achilles heel?'

'I'm a typical Spaniard. Feed me and love me . . . that's all I ask.'

'Ask? Since when have you ever asked for anything? Surely the word is "demand"?'

'Aha, you are learning!' They smiled happily at each other. 'More wine?'

'No . . . I've had plenty, Rafael.' She leaned back in her chair. It had been such a lovely evening. After inspecting the kitchen larder, Alexia had rapidly decided on a cheese omelette and salad, followed by fresh fruit. That decision taken, Rafael had escorted her to her room, carefully emphasising that it was hers, not theirs; his room being down the corridor. He had left her to wash and freshen up, telling her that he would be in the main living room when she felt like joining him.

Her room was enchanting, with painted walls depicting the four seasons. Rafael had said that the walls—frescoes, he had called them—were very old and had been carefully restored a few years ago. A huge bed dominated the room and Alexia had sat on it, bouncing up and down on the supremely comfortable feather mattress.

Slipping off her shirt, she had washed in the little basin in an alcove off the room, before dressing again and opening the French windows which led on to one of the small courtyards.

She resolutely refused to think about her situation. Rafael had given her the opportunity to leave—unspoken, maybe—in the garden of the Castillo. By not leaving she had, in fact, made a decision, and it was not one she really wanted to think about too closely.

Following the sound of music, she had found the large living room, where Rafael was playing on an instrument that she recognised as a harpsichord. He had smiled at her approach, indicating with a nod her glass of wine waiting for her on a small table. His long, slim fingers moved over the keys as he played a Bach toccata.

'Do you like this?' he asked, playing a melody she hadn't heard before. As the notes rang around the room, she found her foot tapping involuntarily.

'What a lovely tune! I don't think I have heard it before.'

'No, you wouldn't have. I've only just written it. I'm glad you like it,' he smiled to himself as he continued to play.

It had been a lovely evening, she thought again as she looked across the kitchen table at Rafael. He had been easy, friendly and amusing. There had been no emotional stress, or sudden rages, and Alexia felt surprisingly warm and relaxed.

She stood up smiling. 'I have enjoyed my day so much,' she said simply. 'I'll just clear away the plates and then I—I think I'd like to—to go to sleep.'

'Of course.' He led her down the corridor, and opened her door. 'I believe there are some spare blankets in the cupboard, should you feel cold. Is there anything else you need?' His voice was calm and friendly, nothing more.

'No . . . er . . . no, I'm fine, thank you.'

'Then I will say goodnight. Sleep well, Alexia.' She was surprised when he merely kissed her hand and left the room. She had been sure that he would . . . well . . . She shook herself mentally. How stupid of her! He had behaved beautifully all day. Surely that was what she wanted. Of course . . . of course it was . . .

She slowly undressed, drawing back the bed cover

and slipping between the cool sheets. Her mind ran back over the day spent in Ronda, quite the nicest day of her Spanish holiday. For some unaccountable reason, sleep wouldn't come and she lay tossing and turning for what seemed hours.

It's just because it's such a hot night, she told herself. It's got nothing to do with ... Her mind skitted off the dangerous subject of Rafael and instead she tried to concentrate on other matters. All to no avail, as constant images of his lovemaking flitted before her closed eyes. She could find no rest as the moonlight poured in through the doors open to the courtyard. She could hear the tinkling of the small fountain, suddenly overwhelmed by a desire for some fresh air to cool her fevered body.

Wrapping the silk bedcover around herself, she slipped through the doors, her feet making no sound on the cool marble floor of the small courtyard. The moonlight streamed down on to the small copper fountain surrounded by its mosaic bowl, as she drifted towards it in the still night. It wasn't until she was almost upon him that she saw Rafael, sitting with his back to her on a stone plinth, watching the cascading water.

Alexia paused and then, as if in a dream, moved slowly forward to stand behind him. He was covered only by a short towel draped around his waist, and his damp hair and the glistening drops of water on his broad back were evidence of his recently having had a shower.

Still in a dreamlike state, she reached out a hand to softly touch his bronzed shoulders with her finger tips. Gently she moved them across his back, her feather-light touch causing him to tremble as he continued to stare fixedly at the fountain.

'*Dios!* Don't—don't tempt me, Alexia!' he groaned in a low, husky voice.

She continued to caress his skin, caught up in the atmosphere of the quiet, moonlit night, helplessly in the grip of an inner force far stronger than her conscious self.

Slowly Rafael reached behind to grasp her arm, drawing her around to face him as he sat on the plinth.

'Are you tempting me?' he breathed softly as he took both her hands in his, gazing intently up into her green eyes.

The silk bedspread, no longer held by her hands, slithered and whispered down her body, falling on to the floor to lie in a shimmering pool about her feet.

'Oh yes, you are indeed tempting me, my Alexia!' his low throbbing voice seemed to come from far away as she stood, still as a statue, aware only of his eyes burning into hers. 'The moonlight has turned you to silver, even your wonderful golden hair,' he murmured slowly with wonder, as he rose to stand looking down at her. 'You know that I love you, my green-eyed witch? That I love you with all my heart?'

'I—I hoped ... I—I wasn't sure ...' she whispered.

'Be very sure, my Alexia.' He bent forward and slowly, almost reverently, picked her up in his strong arms and walked across the marble floor to her room. He lowered her carefully on to the bed as the moon's beam streamed in the open doors, bathing her naked body in a mysterious light.

'You are so lovely, my darling,' he whispered as he gently sat down beside her, stroking the stray locks of hair from her forehead, before his hands cupped her beautiful face as he gazed into her eyes.

Her lips trembled and she gasped, nervously moistened them with the tip of her tongue, as his eyes suddenly changed from gentleness to ardent desire. A slow pulse began to throb in her stomach as he leaned over her, softly brushing her forehead with his lips before trailing them down to kiss the edges of her mouth. Slowly and with infinite care, he teased her lips lightly so that they parted breathlessly under his.

Her arms slowly wound themselves around his neck as she responded to his deepening kiss, her hunger as great as his own. His mouth moved slowly down to the hollow of her throat, her body quivering in response to the delicate caress of his hands as he passed them lightly over her slim shape. His touch gradually became more insistent, his fingers continued to explore every secret part of her body, demandingly possessive as she moaned helplessly at his deliberate arousal of the sensual tide which flowed through every fibre of her being.

He lay looking down at her, his hands caressing her full creamy breasts, swollen with desire. 'So lovely, so lovely,' he murmured thickly, as he devoured her with his eyes in the moonlight.

Scarcely aware of doing so, she removed his rough towel, before moving to softly stroke the curly hair of his chest. 'I love you,' she said, in wonder. 'I love you so much.'

He trembled at her words and touch, as with a deep groan he brought his mouth down to plunder the rosy tips of her breasts. As he murmured softly in Spanish, his ardour increased. Although he tried to restrain his mounting passion, her total sensual abandonment to the touch of his hands and his mouth made it difficult for him to control his leashed strength. Alexia became aware of the increasing urgency of his desire and from the deep mists of her passion, realised she had something to tell him.

'Please,' she whispered. 'Please, I . . . be gentle . . .' but by then it was too late. She screamed—a sharp animal cry—as the pain tore through her body.

'*Dios!*' Rafael's whole body stiffened. Gazing at her in horror, he groaned. '*Esta virgem,* Alexia! Holy Mother of God! You should have told me,' he cried.

'Rafael, I'm so sorry . . . I . . .' The tears trickled down from her frightened eyes.

'Shush, my dearest! I . . . I . . .' He seemed almost lost for words as he comforted her, soothing and stroking her skin, gently kissing her face.

'You love me?' he whispered some time later. 'The worst is over now. You must trust me, yes?' as with infinite patience and skill he began to reawaken all her previous desire. His experienced and masterly touch brought her back to complete sensual abandon, and this time, when she was practically swooning with desire, they came together in a mounting tide of overwhelming passion.

CHAPTER TEN

ALEXIA opened her eyes the next morning to find herself alone in the huge bed. She smiled as she lay back on the pillows, stretching her satiated, languorous body, blushing slightly as she remembered the long passionate night. Twice before dawn Rafael had reached out for her, and each time she had responded wantonly to his tender lovemaking.

She looked up as the door opened and Rafael entered with a tray. He had found a faded blue towelling dressing gown from somewhere, her heart turning over at the sight of his tall, lithe figure. It was only as he turned to face her that she saw his handsome face was set in grim lines. She suddenly began to feel lonely and afraid.

'I'm hopeless in a kitchen,' he said in a hard voice. 'All I could find was some tea-bags—so tea it is.'

Clutching the sheet to her nude body, Alexia struggled to sit up as he handed her a cup. She sat looking down at the pale brown liquid, a deep blush spreading over her features. What happens ... the morning after the night before? she thought in a panic. She had no idea about the rules of an affair. Did one pretend that nothing had occurred?

Her thoughts were interrupted by Rafael's harsh voice. 'Why, in the name of heaven, didn't you tell me that you were a virgin?'

'I ... well, I ...'

'Quite apart from all that crazy jealousy you put me

though, I—I hurt you last night. A hurt that, to a
large extent, could have been avoided.'

She looked up to meet his angry eyes, set in a face
that looked strained and drawn.

'I—I can't explain . . .' she stammered unhappily.

'That's not good enough, and well you know it,
Alexia. Here am I, a brute who took your virginity.
Something I had no right to do!'

'But—you told me you loved me,' she protested
quietly.

'So I do, but that's got nothing to do with the
matter. I would never . . . I mean, it's not right . . . Oh
hell! I—I should have been told!' Rafael ground the
words out savagely.

'How could I tell you that I'd reached almost
twenty-four years of age and never been to bed with a
man?' she pleaded. 'You'd have fallen about laughing!
In this day and age it's like being a—a dodo. I am . . .
er . . . was . . . practically a member of an extinct
species.'

'You should have told me,' he repeated angrily.

'Oh yes,' she said bitterly, the memories of the night
before slowly becoming tarnished by his accusatory
manner. 'I can just see the conversation at dinner.
"Guess what, everybody? I'm a virgin". Really,
Rafael, it's not something one drops casually into a
conversation, is it?'

Despite his self-disgust, he smiled wryly. 'I take
your point. But, my love, we have had several . . . er
. . . passionate interludes in which,' his voice rose,
'you have not only said nothing, but deliberately given
me to understand quite the opposite! "I prefer my
men . . .",' he mimicked with fury.

She blushed. 'Did—did you really believe a word of
it?'

'Well, no, to be honest . . .'

'So who was I supposed to have been to bed with, then?'

'Luis, of course!'

She gasped. 'But, Rafael, you knew . . . from your mother . . . that he was a—a sick man.'

'*Por Dios*, Alexia! How could a man live with you and be able to keep his hands off you? It is not possible . . . look at me last night. I—I knew what I had done to you, and still,' he accused himself harshly, 'yet still twice more in the night, I—I had to possess you. You will have to nail me down in a coffin before I stop wanting you. Luis may have been ill, but no one is that sick!'

'Do you know,' she said, gazing at him dreamily, 'that is . . . absolutely . . . the most wonderful thing anyone has ever said to me.'

'Alexia! This is a serious matter.'

'Rafael,' she said slowly, 'does it . . . does it really matter that much to you? The fact that I hadn't slept with anyone else?'

'Of course.'

'I—I don't see why.'

'How can I explain? I did something wrong . . . really very wrong.'

There was a pause, while she looked at him, the blood draining from her face. 'Are you saying that you—you wouldn't have made love to me last night, if—if you'd known?'

'Yes . . . No . . . I don't know.'

'My God, you—you really do have double standards!'

'*Alexia!*'

'Don't you "Alexia" me! You thought I was secondhand goods, didn't you?' she hissed. 'So it was

all right to have a little fun. You said you loved me . . .
Hah! You didn't mean a damn word of it!'

'Of course I did!'

'Oh no! I was right about you all along. You just
pretended that you loved me, to get me into bed. I—I
bet you say that to all the girls. But you found out I
was that anachronism . . . a virgin. Which is somehow
against your stupid Spanish code of honour . . . and—
and now you feel guilty!'

'Of course I feel guilty!'

'Well, how—how do you think I feel? I feel bloody
awful . . . that's how I feel. I've made a real fool of myself,
haven't I? There was I saying "I love you" like all
your other women . . .' Alexia began to shake with
rage and humiliation. 'I hate you, I hate you!' she
screamed, throwing her cup and saucer at him, almost
beyond herself with fury.

Rafael ducked, as the china hit the wall, falling in
tiny shattered pieces on the floor. Shocked, they
looked at each other in silence.

He sighed and shook his head wearily. 'Alexia,
something has gone very wrong with this conversation. You have entirely misunderstood what I have
been trying to say.' He cleared his throat. 'Yes,
it—it is a serious thing that I did. Very serious. It
is, or should be, a precious thing in a woman. It is
something that should be kept for her marriage. You
were married to Luis, and I—I naturally assumed,
for the reasons I have given, that you and he were
lovers.'

'But . . . I . . .'

'However, the facts are that we made love, that you
were a virgin and therefore we must be married as
soon as possible.'

Alexia looked at him incredulously, her mouth

opening and closing like a fish, while she strove to comprehend what he was saying.

'. . . er . . . let me get this right. Having "taken my virginity", as you put it, you—you now feel you must marry me?'

'I wish to marry you . . . yes.'

'Hang on a minute. You knew immediately when . . . that . . . well, you knew. Which means you've been to bed with some of us virgins before. Right? So how come you didn't marry any of them?'

He smiled, 'You have a beautifully clear and logical mind, *querida!*'

'Don't prevaricate!'

'Oh, my dearest. I—I was younger, and more foolish. Besides, I . . .'

'My God! So now old man Rafael, in his dotage, is going to make an honest woman of one of his conquests. *Fantastic!*'

'What!'

'You heard. Well, I've got news for you. Haven't I just! Nobody, but nobody, has to do me any favours!' Alexia, her large green eyes filled with tears of rage, glared at him with hatred. She couldn't ever remember when she had felt so humiliated and ashamed. 'I'll get married when and how *I* feel like it, and—and it won't be to a randy old man like you, for starters!'

'*Silencio!*' Rafael's face paled as he stared at the tortured girl before him.

'When I marry,' she cried savagely, 'it will be to someone who really loves me. Someone who loves me *because of what I am*, not—not just because he fancies my body, and . . . feels obliged to act the gentleman. Someone who doesn't think he's God's gift to women, and—and doing me a great big favour!'

She paused to take a deep breath, before delivering the most wounding words she could think of as a coup de grâce. '. . . And—and while I'm at it . . . I'll—I'll make sure he's a better lover than you. Which shouldn't be too difficult, if last night was anything to go by!' she shouted.

White as a sheet beneath his tan, Rafael walked slowly, like a leopard after prey, towards the bed.

'So,' he hissed through clenched teeth. 'So . . . you are going to get a better lover, are you? You are going to marry someone else, are you? Well, my dear Alexia,' he purred menacingly, 'I have news for you! You will marry me, and you will enjoy my lovemaking . . . *you understand?*' He stood shaking with rage, regarding her with blazing eyes.

'Get lost!' she cried defiantly. 'I—I wouldn't marry you if you were the last man alive!'

'We'll see about that!' He swiftly whipped the sheet from her trembling hands.

'Stop it! What are you doing? Rafael! . . . leave me alone . . .'

Alexia tried to escape. Scrambling over the bed, she nearly made it to the door before being fielded by Rafael, who threw her back on to the bed with humilating ease. She lay winded for a moment before she rolled off the other side of the mattress, attempting to reach the French windows that led to the courtyard. Striding swiftly Rafael was there before her, tossing her back on to the bed again before ripping off his dressing gown and pinning her to the soft bed with his hard, firm body.

She fought him, wildly and fiercely, for all she was worth; to no avail. Her kicks and struggles were futile against his superior strength, and growing weaker, she began to cry bitter, hopeless tears of frustration and rage.

He lay, his strong wrists like bands of steel on her outstretched arms, as he stared grimly into her tear-filled eyes. 'I told you, the day you arrived in Spain, that you needed taming . . . and so you do! You are mine and will marry me, you understand?'

'No!. she gasped. 'I—I won't! You can't make me . . .'

'Oh yes, I can, Alexia,' he said with a grimly sardonic smile, bringing his hard mouth down on her trembling lips as his hands began to caress her body. She tried not to respond to his erotic lovemaking, but she was powerless in the thrall of his total mastery of her emotions. Sinking under the rising tide of her desire, she was unaware of exactly when she stopped fighting him and began to respond ardently and passionately to the feverishly arousing touch of his mouth and hands, unable to control the sensuous undulations of her body beneath his.

Rafael, on the contrary, had himself totally under control as he brought her to such a pitch of passionate desire that the longing for fulfilment was almost more than she could bear.

'Please . . . Oh, please . . .' she begged.

'You will marry me?' he whispered.

'I . . . Oh, Rafael . . .' Alexia pleaded urgently.

'Say you will marry me,' he demanded harshly.

'Yes . . . yes, I will . . .' she gasped, 'but please . . .' His cry of triumph was the last thing she heard as she lost touch with reality. Drowning in a deeply emotional tide, their two bodies became one as together they scaled the heights of their mutual passion.

She returned to full consciousness to find herself locked in Rafael's arms as he soothed and kissed her brow, damp with perspiration.

'My darling,' he said tenderly, 'how can you doubt that I love you? How can you doubt it?'

She turned her head away, a large tear sliding down her cheek. 'I suppose it's all those—those women, and—and you wouldn't have asked me to marry you if—if I'd been to bed with someone else.'

'Dearest, there has been nobody for me, since the moment I first saw you. You stood looking so—so beautiful and so sad, in that terrible cemetery. Believe me, my darling—I had, and have, every intention of marrying you. Sweet Mother of God! I have thought of nothing else for what seems years, although it is only weeks. I had to wait and hope that you would realise the difference between lust and love. That day on the beach ... you didn't seem to understand what had happened to us ...' He kissed her gently. 'You are such a tough fighter and such a passionate woman. It would have been no good my telling you that I loved you. I—I would merely have frightened you away ...'

He sighed. 'Besides, I was in a devil of a mess. There I was, engaged to Isabella and not seeing how to get out of it. When Rosa found us kissing that day, in your room ...' he laughed wryly. 'She told me to make up my mind! I told her, you were the one—the one I wanted to marry. But having said that, I could not see how to achieve it.'

'She never told me.' Alexia snuggled closer into his arms.

'No ... I threatened her with hell fire and brimstone if she said anything to you. Unfortunately, she told all the servants and even my mother ... *Dios!* It has been like walking on eggshells in the house these last weeks. I thought everything was going to blow up in my face. And then, praise be to God, Isabella fell in love with Michael.'

'I thought you'd be very upset about that. So—so did Isabella. She was a bit miffed that you weren't prostrated with unhappiness.'

'"Miffed"? What an extraordinary English word. Unhappy? *Por Dios*, when I think how I tried to turn that girl against me, without actually being cruel . . .'

'I must say, she always looked very bored with you,' Alexia commented.

'Bored . . . I can't begin to tell you how boring I tried to be! When she told me about Michael, I could hardly contain my joy.'

'But you told her that you had no wish to marry, ever. That you were wedded to your career,' she quizzed him lovingly.

'Well, I had to say something to save her face, didn't I? I owe Michael a great deal, and I must buy one of his computers for my new farm. I hope and pray they are tucked up in bed right now.'

'Rafael!'

'Why not? We are.'

'I tried not to be jealous, but she—she is so beautiful.'

'Yes, she is, but she is a bore. I was never in love with her, and besides, one cannot love to order. I didn't want to love you, you maddening girl. No—not at all!'

'Especially when you thought I was a loose woman!'

He groaned. 'You will never let me forget that, will you? I must have been out of my mind at the time. Really *loco*! I couldn't keep my hands off you, even in London . . . and so jealous of poor Luis. It was terrible of me to be so envious of him.'

'I've never understood why Luis was estranged from the family,' Alexia confessed.

'Luis was four years younger than I and very, very serious.' Rafael sighed unhappily. 'Did you know that he wished to enter the Church . . . to be a priest?'

'No! I—I had no idea. Really?'

'Oh yes. Always, from a boy. When I made the choice to leave my studies and sing for money, it was a shock to my family. Some of my relations—well, they were scandalised that such a thing could happen. By the time everything was starting to go well with my career, Luis, aged about twenty, had joined a seminary.' Rafael's dark eyes clouded at the recollection. 'Unfortunately he was teased by the others there, about me and the women who liked my singing. At the same time he lost his faith. Somehow, I do not really understand why, the two matters became muddled in his head and he blamed me and my profession. He was very unhappy.'

'Oh, Rafael, I'm so sorry. Poor Luis,' she said. 'I had no idea he had been so religious. I suppose he was a Catholic? I—I buried him in a Protestant grave, was that wrong of me?'

'Of course not. God is God. He sees and knows all. Anyway, Luis did agree to meet me in London, when he told me all about your sister. I was hopeful, but after that . . . nothing.' Rafael shrugged despondently.

'Oh, my darling, please don't blame yourself,' Alexia comforted him. 'When Antonia died, he no longer wanted to live, truly he didn't.'

'I understand that now, but I have felt a heavy burden of guilt about him for a long time. Which is why, I suspect, I was so angry when I first met you.'

'Yes, you were.' Alexia snuggled closer in his arms. 'Really very nasty indeed. And . . . well, kissing me like that! I'd—I'd never been kissed in that way before, I was terribly shocked and upset and. . . .'

'*Deseo de mi corazon*—my heart's desire, Alexia, *mi bella amada*,' he whispered softly as his mouth possessed her lips.

'For heaven's sake, Rafael!' she gasped weakly before silence descended, only broken by occasional gentle murmurs in Spanish.

'You . . . you're incorrigible!' Alexia sat up, smiling breathlessly. 'That's why I don't trust you. How do I know you really want to marry me . . . and not because of some crazy nonsense about your Spanish honour?'

He grinned sheepishly. 'Dearest, I had to strike when the opportunity arose. I—I was planning to ask you tonight, after the concert. But I was so upset at hurting you needlessly, I . . .' he groaned, burying his face in her soft breasts.

'Oh, my darling,' she sighed, cradling his head, 'I'll always be so jealous of all those women of yours!'

He looked up. 'How do I know that you love me, Alexia? How can I trust you with all those men, like Pierre and Jerry?' He ground his teeth. 'I will not have you flirting with that Frenchman again—white roses indeed! I can see that we must be married very soon, if I am to have any peace of mind.'

'Of course, you can trust me, but . . . but you and all those women . . . it's different . . .' she tried to explain.

'No, it's not. I know I love you, and I know I will be true to you. You must trust me . . . we must trust each other, *querida*.'

'There's another thing,' she said with a worried frown. 'We're going to fight a lot, aren't we?'

'Oh yes,' he said cheerfully, 'I'm sure we are.'

'But aren't you worried about it?'

'No—why should I be? I can master you, *mi* Alexia, any time I wish to.'

'Well! Of all the damn, arrogant . . .'

'*Bastante!* Enough! Yes, I will be your master, my darling, shout at me as you will . . . *Dios!*' he laughed, 'you certainly will give me a hard time!'

'Will I be expected to sit at home and have babies, while you gallivant all over the globe? *Heavens!* I'd forgotten all about my business, Rafael. I can't leave that. Really I can't. I've worked so hard and . . .'

'Alexia, calm down. Firstly, yes, I hope you will have babies. We shall enjoy making them, will we not? Secondly, I told you last night that I am giving up singing. So we will live here in Ronda, and be very happy.' He kissed her gently. 'However, you must listen very carefully to what I say now. You must understand that I am not prepared to compromise on your life with your computers. If you marry me, they will have to go. You will be my wife—first and last— and that is very definitely that!'

'Oh, Rafael!' she cried, looking at his stern, unrelenting features, her green eyes filled with dismay.

'*Querida*, I am very, very serious about this. My love for you is very fierce, very strong,' he said huskily. 'But I am also a very selfish, possessive man. So, my lovely Alexia, you must make up your mind either to marry me, or go back to London and resume your life with your floppy disks.'

'Not even a little part-time . . .'

'*Absolutamente, no!*' he said firmly.

Alexia looked hard and long at Rafael, her eyes searching his impassive face for some sign of weakness. She sighed, 'You . . . you know very well that nothing—nothing's worth a damn . . . not if I can't have you, Rafael.' She shrugged with resignation.

'All right, you win. I'll—I'll close down my business.'

'*Te quiero,* my adorable Alexia!' He smiled lovingly at her, drawing her closely into his arms. 'I may be possessive but I am not, I hope, a cruel man.' he murmured, covering her face with kisses. 'You have a good brain, and should use it. When I was away in Madrid making my latest record, I . . . er . . . I bought the record company. I will make you one of the directors, yes? We will see just how good you are at business—hm?'

'Oh, Rafael!' She threw her arms around him. 'How lovely . . . what fun!'

'But you must never forget that I insist—arrogant or not—I insist that I, and our children, will come first. You will have to manage that . . . or no business. You understand?'

'Yes,' she whispered, raising her lips to his. 'I'll always put you first, my dearest, dearest Rafael.'

'So—you definitely agree to marry me?'

'Well, taking the rough with the smooth, all in all, I suppose . . .'

He took her laughing face in his hands. 'How I love you, my green-eyed girl. How I love you!'

'Oh, Rafael, I love you so much, it—it frightens me sometimes,' she confessed.

'I understand, because I feel the same way, my darling. You will see,' he kissed her passionately. 'Soon I hope you will see. Come,' he said reluctantly, 'we must get back. I have a lot to do before tonight and you must see Juan. Ha! I will be a father very soon. I shall have a son as soon as we marry!'

'Darling, he'll be so happy. Oh, my God! I've just thought . . . your mother! What will she think?'

'Darling,' he laughed, 'this idyll of ours was suggested by Mamá. She said we had got ourselves into such knots, and we were both too proud to even begin trying to untie them. She is a wise woman, no?'

'Yes, she is. But she can't have expected us to . . . well, here in bed!'

'She did not mention that specifically, but as she suggested we had a nice quiet dinner and stayed the night, I imagine she had some idea of the situation, don't you?'

'I'll never be able to look her in the face again.' Alexia blushed.

'Oh yes, you will. We must hurry up and get dressed. Do not forget, while I am out of the room for the next five minutes, that I love you. I will try and prove it to you—be patient.'

Later that evening in the bullring, as Alexia sat in the President's box with Doña Maria and Julia either side of her, he did prove it . . . in his own way.

It took Alexia some time to reconcile the tall charismatic figure on the stage with the Rafael she knew. Dressed in a pair of slim-fitting white trousers, worn with a loose white silk shirt with large, full sleeves and clasped at his waist in a wide gold belt; he dominated the audience with his commanding stage presence even before he began to sing his first song. He's holding them all in the palm of his hand, she thought, looking around the large arena, filled to capacity and even overflowing as people tried to squeeze in to the standing-room-only corridors at the back of the seats.

She had only seen Rafael sing on television, the day of Luis's funeral, and seated at a piano at Jerry's party. His stage act was a revelation as he moved fluidly around the stage, weaving in and out amongst the musicians, totally master of his performance and of the capacity crowd.

He sang song after song, some fast and lilting, some slow and sad, the audience going mad with applause and shouts of 'Raf-a-el ... Raf-a-el!' between each number. Alexia was surprised to see some women in the next box crying hysterically, their arms outstretched as he sang the haunting melody he had composed for her: 'Who Are You, What are you—you have bewitched me'. That tune received special applause, almost certainly destined for the top ten of the charts.

The performance was drawing to a close, when the lights dimmed and Rafael came forward to make an announcement. Alexia couldn't follow his Spanish, but when the music started she recognised the tune. It was the one he had played on the harpsichord last night.

The drummer started an incessant disco beat, which was taken up by the guitarists, while Rafael stood silently beside a musician who stepped forward to a microphone and began to play the melody on a clarinet. Slowly, Rafael began to join his voice to that of the instrument, his lyrical tones harmonising with the clarinet in a warm, melodious serenade. No one present that night was in any doubt whatever that they were listening to something special. In the years to come, they would remind their friends of the occasion on which they had first heard the melody, the tune that was to become one of the great modern songs of the twentieth century.

Alexia thought that some of the Spanish words sounded like her name, but dismissed such a silly idea as she sat enchanted, listening as Rafael's voice soared in unison with the clarinet, only gradually becoming distracted by the people in her box who were turning to smile at her.

'How romantic it is,' Julia giggled, giving her a nudge. 'He must love you very much!'

'What?' Alexia gazed at the girl, completely mystified. Suddenly a spotlight hit their box, and she was bathed in the glow of a brilliant incandescence.

She looked around, startled, to see everyone clapping and laughing as over the loudspeaker, Rafael serenaded her, in English:

'Sweet Alexia——
Without your love I cannot live—Oh, my heart!
Sweet Alexia——'
Give me your love that I may live—in your heart!
Sweet Alexia—
Accept my love and together we shall live—in my heart.'

The music died slowly away as Rafael stepped forward and bowed to her. Pushed to her trembling feet by Doña Maria, she moved like a sleepwalker to the front of the box, still bathed by the spotlight, while the audience broke into a mad orgy of applause.

Smiling across the mass of people, seeing only the face of the man she loved, Alexia watched as a way was formed to allow Rafael to approach and stand, laughing with happiness, before her.

'Oh, Rafael, I—I do believe you love me. I really do!' she cried joyfully, bending forward to kiss him.

As they embraced, the crowd erupted with frenzied clapping and wild shouts of '*Olé! Olé!*' the oldest and greatest cry of the bullring, awarded when the matador . . . having given a masterly performance by displaying his finesse and courage in the contest . . . triumphantly claims his reward.

Share the joys and sorrows
of real-life love with
Harlequin American Romance! ™·

GET THIS BOOK
FREE as your introduction to
Harlequin American Romance —
an exciting series of romance
novels written especially for
the American woman of today.

Mail to:
Harlequin Reader Service

In the U.S.
2504 West Southern Ave.
Tempe, AZ 85282

In Canada
P.O. Box 2800, Postal Station A
5170 Yonge St., Willowdale, Ont. M2N 5T5

YES! I want to be one of the first to discover
Harlequin American Romance. Send me FREE and without
obligation *Twice in a Lifetime*. If you do not hear from me after I
have examined my FREE book, please send me the 4 new
Harlequin American Romances each month as soon as they
come off the presses. I understand that I will be billed only $2.25
for each book (total $9.00). There are no shipping or handling
charges. There is no minimum number of books that I have to
purchase. In fact, I may cancel this arrangement at any time.
Twice in a Lifetime is mine to keep as a FREE gift, even if I do not
buy any additional books.   154 BPA NAVY

Name   (please print)

Address   Apt. no.

City   State/Prov.   Zip/Postal Code

Signature (If under 18, parent or guardian must sign.)

This offer is limited to one order per household and not valid to current Harlequin
American Romance subscribers. We reserve the right to exercise discretion in
granting membership. If price changes are necessary, you will be notified.

Offer expires March 31, 1985

AMR-SUB-1